Splinters

SPLINTERS

CHRIS JEAL

Bad Egg Publishing

First Published in Great Britain 2018 by Bad Egg Publishing

badeggpublishing@gmail.com

Cover art by Ben White.

ISBN 9781999612214

CONTENTS

Acknowledgments	vii
Introduction	1
Shenanigans	3
The Heartbreak Police	8
Broken Home	23
Sick Puppy	33
The Boy with Cogs for a Heart	37
Toilet	43
A Good Wife	45
The Night Bus	50
#MegaLolz	59
The Handyman	61
The Little Shop of Revenge	69
PIG	76
Meat Ben	83
The Bad Slice	93

ACKNOWLEDGMENTS

Thanks and Acknowledgments

Vix who is just the bestest. Rich Brown, a fantastic writer who has helped me immensely with feedback and advice. Declan Taaffe for all his support and encouragement. And of course, the people at Create50. Without their Twisted50 competition, I would never have ventured down this path and Splinters would not exist. A special thanks to Cristina Palmer-Romero, and also to Chris Jones for allowing me to include Shenanigans, Pig and The Little Shop of Revenge in this collection.

You can contact me at badeggpublishing@gmail.com
Or follow me on Twitter @ChrisJeal

Chris.

INTRODUCTION

When I was seven, I used to stay at my nan's every Friday night. Around eight o'clock the 'video lady' would visit us. The video lady wasn't some ghostly apparition, but a tall crazy-haired woman, who, every weekend, would drive around the estate loaded up with laundry bags crammed with VHS tapes for rent. She was like a mobile Blockbuster video, with an old beat-up white van instead of a vibrant shop front.

She would come into nan's house smelling of stale tobacco, dragging huge bags bursting with tapes. One night, I ran down the stairs to meet her and did that strange dance kids do when they're overexcited (the one where they throw their arms about like a marionette operated by a drunk.) The video lady hefted the bags to the centre of the hallway and straightened up. 'Only got cartoons and kid's stuff this week,' she said pulling a cigarette from a crumpled pack, popping it into her mouth and lighting up.

I stopped dancing.

She pinched the cigarette from her lips and blew smoke into the air, 'Just kidding,' she said. 'I got all kinds of lunatics and ghoulies with me tonight.'

For years she'd come to my nan's every Friday, and I'd be allowed to pick a tape. One week it would be about a monster terrorising a group of kids, the next about a man with a split personality and a taste for murder. Each video was a look into another world, a story that would stay with me well after the weekend.

It was those films, those stories that made me want to tell my own.

Fast forward many years and here I am at your door with Splinters, my own bag of horrors and weird things in book form. I don't expect you to do the 'excited' dance (you're an adult now) and don't worry about having to pick just one, as all of these belong to you now. You don't even need a VHS player, just a quiet place to escape to for a while.

Are you ready? That's good, because I got all kinds of lunatics and ghoulies with me tonight...

SHENANIGANS

I get into my car and sink into the plush leather of the driver's seat. Placing my mobile phone on the dash, I take a deep breath and enjoy that new car smell. It's great to finally be able to have the things I've always wanted – even if it has cost me a lot more than just money. The phone's screen lights-up and a jaunty voice calls out. "Hey John, you slow-poke. You now only have three hours left to complete Shenanigan: *Bloody Heartbreaker.*" This is the Host, the voice of The App and possibly that of the Devil himself, or maybe something much, much worse...

I jam the keys into the ignition, fire up the engine and drive away into the night.

Thirteen months, that's how long The App has been around and five of those months was all it took for society to break down and take a shit on itself – The App changed everything. No one knows who created it, or where it originated but on Tuesday 22nd June 2016 it appeared on everyone's phone, tablet and laptop. Every network, every town, every country got The App. At first, people thought it was a scam, *one weird trick to make you rich,* but when they realized it was legit and they saw what it offered, people went crazy for it... literally.

The App offers cash prizes to perform dares, or *Shenanigans* as the Host calls them. Pick a Shenanigan from the list, film it, upload the footage and the money is transferred to your account – simple as that. The dares started pretty tame, with things like *Eat Worms!* which paid £50.00 or *Slap a Friend!* for £80.00. Once people got into the swing of it and the money started pouring in, things escalated rapidly. *Eat Worms!* changed to *Eat Glass! Slap a Friend!* turned to *Mutilate a Friend*!

I steer onto the common and pass through what was once a thriving neighbourhood, now everything looks like it's been chewed up and spat out. The police can't stop it, and the few officers who still patrol the streets are more likely to commit Shenanigans than prevent them. If you did get arrested, it's doubtful you'd make it back to the station.

Headlights pick out movement in the road up ahead. I stamp the brakes and crunch gravel, grinding to a halt in front of two scabby women dragging a barely conscious blood-covered man across the road. One of them points at me with the fleshy stump of her arm. *Probably did that to herself.* Mutilation and self-mutilation Shenanigans equal big payouts – a year's wage to hack off a limb is a reasonable proposition for those who are desperate. I grab my phone and check the Shenanigans list to see if I can make some cash by flattening these fucks into the gravel – I quickly change my mind as I consider the mess it'll make of the new car. I palm the horn. "Get the fuck outta the way." They scurry off into the darkness with their prize, no doubt taking him somewhere to indulge in some slice 'n' dice.

I drive on.

Things have gotten even more interesting since the new app-upgrade: The App 2.0. Now Shenanigans are streamed live as the Host offers bonuses and cash multipliers to encourage you to get even more creative and twisted. The first time I witnessed 2.0, I was in the supermarket. I turned into the frozen goods aisle and walked into a Shenanigan in progress, a man was beating a screaming blonde woman to the floor. When he'd knocked the fight out of her and she was choking on her own teeth, he started tearing at her clothes. The Host called out from the man's phone. "Make it multiplayer! 10X the cash if you make it a party! Have fun with it. Share with friends!" People who had been watching didn't take much persuading to wade in on her too – everyone has a price – and it wasn't long before it was a game with twelve players. When they'd finished with her, Blondie's limp body was dumped in with the frozen potato waffles. Sure, someone could have intervened, tried to save her, but who'd pass up that kind of cash? And those that didn't get involved? They were too busy with their heads down, checking The App for an 'easier' Shenanigan – these people are in denial, thinking they'll just take on the tame stuff. But it doesn't take long for your moral compass to fracture and you're doing the real nasty shit.

I pull up at Kenbrook flats, kill the engine and once more take in that new car smell. I tap The App, and speak into my phone. "This is John Glenn, going live with Shenanigan: *Bloody Heartbreaker*."

"Make this your best Shenanigan yet, Tiger," chirps the Host. "Remember to use your official App gear for bonuses and multipliers!" I open the glove box and pull out my official App *Shenani-cam* retina recorders™. These are awesome, contact lenses that record everything. Some people still use head cams. Amateurs. I slip the retina recorders over my eyes and check my other gear, all bought from in-app pop-ups and advertising. I have my App *Scream For Me slice-'n'-dice* knife™', my official App *I Can't Feel My Legs!* restraints™' and my 'App *Deepest itch* internal flayer™' Using all these official items brings bigger bonuses and multipliers. I simply refuse to use any other brand.

I pocket my phone, bag my gear and bail from the car. I

make my way to the tower block entrance and key in the door code, all the while keeping an eye out for anyone who might be looking to Shenanigan me.

Inside, I take the lift.

A *ping* announces my arrival at the top floor and the doors clatter open. I step out and make my way towards a reinforced door protected by security bars. "Let's get messy, mah boy!' the Host shouts from my mobile. "Don't puss out!" *No way. Not me.* I knock on the door, after a moment a voice calls from the other side. "Who is it?"

"It's me." Locks slide and chains clang. The door opens, Tanya stands there looking delicious in a stunning evening dress. "Well look at you," I grin. I enter, kissing her as I pass, looking at the bandaged stump where her arm used to be. She's been such a good girlfriend, that arm paid for my new car.

I rock down the hallway towards the kitchen. The taste of Tanya fizzes on my lips and for a second I wonder how much of a multiplier I could rack-up if I fried and ate a bit of her.

Inside the kitchen, candlelight hugs flutes filled with champagne and casts shadows on a table laid with a beautiful spread – I love date night.

I place my bag down and wonder whether to start with some genital mutilation to get things rolling. I'm thinking I can earn at least fou–*A sharp pain in my lower back.* For a second I feel like I've shit myself as my trousers flood with hot liquid. I look at my feet. Blood pools around them. *Oh shit.* I stumble back, crashing to the floor. Tanya looms over me clutching a knife, wearing a small camera strapped to her head. It's nowhere near as cool as my *Shenani-Cam Retina Recorders*™ and I snort at how stupid she looks. I splutter, "How did you –"

"– Know that you were coming to torture me and be a *Bloody Heartbreaker,* John? You're really behind with your tech." She pulls her phone from her pocket and holds it up for me to see. "The new App 3.0 + alerts me when anyone in my contacts list accepts a Shenanigan."

3.0?!? How could I have missed this?

Tanya taps the phone's screen and holds it to her mouth. "This is Tanya Morrison, high-jacking *Bloody Heartbreaker* from John Glenn."

"Well this is an exciting turn, Tanya! Make that no good scallywag scream!" Tanya stalks toward me with the knife.

"Whoa! Bonus Alert! Thirty thousand if you cut off his winky and feed it to him."

Tanya smiles. "Accepted." She eyes my crotch. "Grilled or fried, John?"

I look at the candlelit grin of the blade. "Wait!" I shout. Tanya pauses, unimpressed. I continue. "That isn't an official App knife… use the knife in my bag… it'll up your multiplier."

A warm smile spreads across Tanya's face. "You are always so sweet, John. Doing this is gonna break my bloody heart."

THE HEARTBREAK POLICE

Big Frank poured coffee into a mug with the words *I'm the Boss* printed on it. He looked out over the reception desk and scanned the empty waiting room. His gaze flicked from the dating-advice magazines stacked neatly on the corner table, to the well-kept spider plants flanking the main entrance. He looked at the pools of light from the overhead striplights reflected in the shiny linoleum. The floor didn't really need it, but he considered dragging the buffer from the cupboard and giving it a whirl to ease the monotony of a slow night.

Frank sipped his coffee and turned to observe Charlie sat at his desk. The old man had his head buried in a fishing magazine, his feet up, his trousers halfway up his shins displaying two odd socks and skinny white legs.

'Quiet night,' Frank muttered.

'Yip,' replied Charlie without a glance in Frank's direction. 'Yep. Quiet indeed.'

Frank took another sip of coffee. A half-slurp escaped his mouth and splashed down a metal badge on his blazer that read: Heartbreak Police.

Bang!

Frank jerked, spilling more coffee on himself as the entrance doors flew open with such force they gave the spider plants concussion. A young man, with bloodshot eyes, staggered forward clutching his chest. He swayed left and right, like a cowboy in a western who'd just taken a bullet. Frank straightened up, thumbed coffee from his badge and placed both palms on the desk. 'All the way up to the desk please, sir. Not far now,' he encouraged.

The young man zig-zagged several more times, before slamming into Frank's desk. The impact caused the young man's meticulously constructed flop of blonde hair to flap down over his puffy red face. 'It hurts so much,' he whimpered as an eager bead of snot raced from his nostril and pooled on the well-polished wood of Frank's work area.

Frank opened a drawer, removed a box of tissues and a leather-bound book with *'Incidents'* written on the cover. He pushed the box towards the young man who took a tissue and emptied a thunderous wad of snot into it. Frank took one too, dealt with the coffee stain on his top, cleaned up the snot pool and discarded the wad in the bin at his feet. He pulled a pen from his top pocket, opened the incidents book and cleared his throat.

'Name please, young man.'

'Sam.'

Frank began writing in the book. 'And why are we seeing you tonight, Sam?'

'I think she's ripped my heart out,' he whined. 'My heart!'

'Okay, Sam. Take it easy, please. Would you open your jacket for me so I can take a look?'

Sam nodded floppily, like a child whose head was too heavy for his neck. He stepped away from the desk and slowly unzipped his jacket. 'I'm telling you,' he blubbed. 'You've not seen anything like this before. It's the worst.' Sam pulled his jacket open and revealed the problem – a bloody hole in his chest the size of a dinner plate, the creamy white bones of his ribcage snapped and splintered, the coronary arteries squirting and thrashing like unmanned firehouses, trying to feed a heart that wasn't there.

Unfazed, Frank took notes. He looked over his shoulder to Charlie. 'What do you think?' he asked.

Charlie looked up from his magazine and squinted. 'Yeap, heart's been ripped out, alright,' he muttered before going back to an article about bait.

Sam flopped onto the desk. 'Oh, God. I can't believe she'd do this to me.'

'Foolish,' Charlie said without looking up.

Sam jabbed a finger in Charlie's direction. 'Hey, you don't know how it feels. She was special.'

'Yep, you're the only one who's ever felt like this,' said Charlie, his head still buried in the magazine. 'You're a special little flower.'

'Okay, that's enough,' interrupted Frank. He offered Sam a smile. 'I'm sorry about him. Let's continue. If you prefer we could do this sitting down?'

'No, no. I can't sit down.' Sam shook his head, his flop of blonde hair whipping left and right. Frank didn't know what style this was, but it looked to him like the barber gave up halfway through.

'Okay, so-'

Drip.

Drip.

Drip.

Frank leant over the desk. Sam's shirt was drenched with blood and hung heavy on his hips, dripping on to the clean floor. Sam pawed at the mess of his chest and held up two red palms. 'I'm dying.'

'I know it feels bad now, Sam. But I assure you, it will

get better.' Frank looked back to Charlie. 'Get a tray for the gentleman, please.'

Charlie didn't budge.

'Charlie, now please.'

With a huff, Charlie threw down his magazine. He kicked back his chair and marched over to a large steel cabinet. He threw open the doors and rummaged inside pulling out a silver tray that dazzled under the bright lights. He marched over to the reception desk and dropped it over the side next to Sam. It clattered and clanged at his feet.

'Thank you, Charlie,' said Frank. 'Kindly stand in that, Sam. It will collect any spillage.' Charlie stomped back to his desk, plonked himself back in his chair and snatched up his magazine.

Sam stepped into the tray. He watched in horror as bright red blood pooled around his feet.

'I know it looks bad now, but we're going to help you through this,' said Frank. 'Can you tell me what happened?'

Sam steeled himself. 'Sure. I… I was at the wine bar with friends. I left early and went to Natasha's house… to surprise her,' Sam paused, trying to fight back the next wave of tears. 'And then…'

'Please continue, Sam. You're doing really well.'

Sam gulped and spat the words out chain gun fast, 'I caught them in bed together, her and my best friend they were all over each other it was awful.' He slumped forward and rested his head on the counter.

'That's why the wound is so bloody. You've suffered a double betrayal,' said Frank. He jotted more notes in the Incidents book. 'Have you ever had your heart ripped out before?'

Sam lifted his head and looked at Frank through pain-marinated eyes. 'N… no, I haven't,' he sniffed and straightened up. 'Are you sure she's ripped it out? Maybe she's just broken it a little,' he asked, a hint of optimism in his voice.

'Sorry, Sam but if it was a broken heart, it would simply have a crack down the middle.' Frank pointed his pen towards Sam's gooey chest cavity. 'Yours is not where it should be. It has been ripped out.'

'The bitch.' Sam whipped another tissue from the box and snorted the contents of his nose into it. 'How could she do this to me? We were soul mates.'

'How long was the relationship?' Frank asked.

'Two weeks,' Sam croaked.

Frank's pen slowed.

Charlie looked up from his magazine with an expression usually reserved for those who'd eaten shit.

'Two weeks?' Frank placed his pen down. 'Two weeks? You gave a girl your heart after two weeks?'

'Yeah, yeah. So what?' said Sam becoming more and more animated. 'Two weeks. Two weeks. What's wrong with that?'

'Why did you make such a big investment so early?' asked Frank.

'Because he's a snot-nosed kid, who doesn't know his arse from his elbow. That's why,' Charlie offered.

'Hey, screw you, old man.' Sam bolted out of the tray and leant over the desk, glaring at Charlie.

'Please, Sam. Back in the tray,' said Frank. He turned to Charlie and held out an opened palm like you would to a loyal but mean old mutt. 'Charlie, please keep it to yourself.'

'Well, kids, running around thinking they know about love. They know nothing. They think using mobile phones and hash browns to find love is how it works.'

'It's hashtags, Charlie, and they don't work that way,' replied Frank.

'You know how I met my wife, June, God rest her soul? Serendipity. We were in the tackle shop looking for bait, and we bumped into each other. The maggots went all over the place, and as we both bent down to pick up the wriggly little bastards, we banged hea–'

'I don't think you're helping, Charlie. Can we stick to company practice, please?' Frank didn't disagree with Charlie, serendipity *was* definitely dead. It had been bludgeoned over the head and dumped in the gutter by technology.

'You don't know what we had together,' said Sam. 'We had our own way of seeing the world. We had little in-jokes.'

Charlie snorted. 'You think just because someone laughs at the dumb stuff that comes out of your face, it's love?'

'Is this how this place works?' Sam eyeballed Frank. 'Aren't you supposed to be sorting this out?'

'Charlie, put the kettle on, please,' Frank asked.

Charlie slapped his magazine down. 'Gladly, if I don't have to listen to this rubbish.' He stormed away and disappeared into a side room.

Frank smiled. 'I'm sorry about him. He's been here too long, and he's... well, he's mean. He's a mean old fart, that's what he is.'

'There's no need for it. I'm hurting here,' Sam said, poking at his exposed ribcage.

'I know, I know. Look, two weeks? Okay, it's not long, but it's the journey, not the mileage, eh?'

Sam nodded. 'Yeah, exactly.' He wiped his eyes. 'You'll help me get her back now?'

Frank leant over the desk and placed a sympathetic hand on Sam's shoulder. 'I'm afraid things don't work like that here, Sam. We offer ways to get over the pain, not win her back. We're not going to drive you to the airport to stop her catching that flight, or–'

'What? She's at the airport?' Sam shouted. 'Jesus Christ, I've got to stop her.'

'No, no, calm down. She's not at the airport. It's just a little example I use. Like in films, where the boy chases after the girl to tell her he loves her.'

Sam calmed. 'Oh,' he said, looking embarrassed. He stroked his hair back into place and wiped his nose with the back of his hand. 'You mean like in rom-coms?'

'Yes, romantic comedies,' replied Frank.

A wall of tears covered Sam's eyes. 'We loved watching films together. We were FilmFlix buddies.' He let out a long whine that mimicked a whistling kettle reaching the boil. 'FilmFlix and chill,' he whispered to himself, 'FilmFlix… and chill.'

'There, there,' Frank said, hiding how tired he was of hearing about "FilmFlix and chill". These were exactly the sort of cases that had made Charlie the old curmudgeon he was today. Years ago people suffered hardship and relationships were forged; you'd endure the hard times together and come out stronger – Old Love was forged. New Love was streamed, subscribed and swiped right.

'So… so what's next?' asked Sam, pulling Frank from his thoughts.

'We look at ways to assuage the situation. Make it bearable for you.' Frank ducked behind the counter and banged about. Three bangs and a bonked head later, he reappeared cradling a fluffy grey kitten. He sat it on the desk in front of Sam. The kitten looked up with cute blue eyes and let out an adorable *meow*.

'Huh? I don't get it.' Sam scratched his head.

Frank stroked the kitten's tiny head. 'You have to fill the

hole she left with something new until the pain becomes bearable.' The kitten purred and nudged Frank's hand, desperate for more strokes.

'How does this help me?'

'Something else to focus on, take your mind off of the relationship ending.' Frank carefully scooped up the kitten and held it towards Sam. 'Hold your jacket open, please. Let's see if it helps.' Sam reluctantly opened his jacket. Frank leant over the counter and inserted the purring ball of fluff into the sucky chest-cavity. He slid his hands away, leaving the kitten on the top of Sam's heaving lungs – the cat did a three-sixty and settled down, curling up into a ball.

The sound of satisfied purrs crackled in Sam's chest. 'It tickles.'

'How does that feel?'

'It feels weird. I mean, there's a kitten where my heart should be.'

'Yes, I know, but isn't it better than having *nothing* where your heart should be? It feels nice, right, taking your mind off things?'

'I guess, but not really in a good way. Only in the way that there's an animal sleeping in my guts.' Sam became agitated. His hands waved in the air and he fidgeted on the spot like an infant needing a wee.

'Okay, that's fine,' said Frank. 'Come on, Battle Cat.' The kitten yawned and stretched. Frank extended his arms and Battle Cat hopped out of Sam's chest, into the palm of his hand. The cat strolled lazily up his arm and settled on his shoulder. 'Okay, moving on. Let's try something else. Dog lover maybe?' Frank ducked behind the counter.

'No. No animals, please.'

Frank straightened up. 'That's fine. We've got plenty of other things we can try.' He walked over to the cabinet at the back of the room. He opened it up and rattled around inside and heaved out a laden wooden toolbox. He carried it over to Sam and banged it down on the desk.

Sam's eyes widened at all the sharp tools jutting out of it. 'What the hell? I'm not putting that in my chest.'

'You don't put them in the cavity. You use them to start a project.'

'A project?'

Frank opened his drawer and pulled out a binder bursting with documents. 'Yes, a project. Build something.' He opened the binder and flicked through the pages, each one containing detailed instructions on how to assemble various things. 'You could build a spice rack.' Frank flicked to another page. 'A shelf.' and then another. 'Ooh, this is a good one, birdhouse. Build a nice birdhouse for all the–'

'Birds, yeah, I get it. Why would I want to do any of that?'

Before Frank could answer, the entrance doors slid open. A tall, pale man dressed in a black trench coat, carrying a briefcase, sauntered into the room. He held out a wet umbrella and shook it over Frank's shiny floor. 'It's raining cats and dogs out there,' the man declared with a grin – he eyeballed the kitten on Frank's shoulder and jabbed the umbrella in its direction. 'Seems you have a leak.'

The kitten hissed. Frank patted the feline's head. 'It's okay, BC'

The pale man made a beeline for Sam. He extended a leather-gloved-hand for the shaking. 'Good evening, pleased to you. My name is Archie Kellum, and I'm a Heart-Break Prevention Specialist.' Archie grasped Sam's hand, his leather gloves squeaking as they shook.

'You don't have to talk to this man, Sam. He doesn't represent this company,' said Frank.

Kellum eyed the toolbox on the counter. 'Still pushing

spice racks and pets on the emotionally ravaged youth of today, Frank? So out of touch.'

Battle Cat bared his tiny teeth and pushed out a *hiss*.

Archie blew a raspberry back at him. 'The YOLO generation need more than what you can offer them, Frank. It's a war zone of love out there these days.'

'It's standar–'

'Yes standard, standard boring standard,' said Archie waving unenthused jazz hands to hammer home his disdain. 'Steve, here–'

'Sam,' corrected Sam.

'Of course, Sam here needs an expert.' Archie placed his hand on the boy's shoulder and pulled him closer. 'You don't want to take advice from someone who thinks Tinder is something you take camping. He–'

'You can leave now, Kellum,' said Frank.

Kellum whipped his arm away and feigned offence. 'Why I'm just eager to help someone in need. I'm not causing any trouble. We're just two men about town wagging chins aren't we, Sam?'

'Err, yeah. It's fine,' said Sam, pushing hair from his face.

Frank rolled his eyes.

'You're going to love this, Sam,' Kellum said, swinging his briefcase onto the counter. He flicked the latches, lifted the lid and spun it around for Sam to see. 'What do you think?' Sam's jaw dropped and his eyelids peeled back – inside the red velvet-lined case, was a beating heart, its surface not a vibrant red but black as coal.

Badoom, badoom.

Badoom, badoom.

Badoom, badoom.

The muscle beat louder and louder, the veins pulsed as

blood surged through them. Battle Cat shuffled along Frank's shoulder and hid in the nook of his neck.

'What is it?' asked Sam, eyes locked on the heart.

'This is the original cold, black heart. It doesn't do *feelings;* it can't be broken.' Kellum reached inside and yanked it from the case. He held it out to Sam, presenting it as if it were some kind of priceless treasure. 'Here, take it. Feel how powerful it is,' Kellum cooed.

Sam reached out and just as his fingers teased the slick of its surface, Kellum whipped the heart away from him and dropped it. Kellum booted the pumping muscle high into the air and across the room. It bounced off the wall and deflected towards the ceiling where it hit between the tube-lights with a meaty splat that left a black mark. The heart fell back to earth – Kellum leapt up and snatched it from the air. He hoisted it above his head and grinned at Sam. 'It doesn't break or get damaged like those silly regular hearts.' Kellum leant in and whispered. 'No one could rip this beast out.' He placed the heart into Sam's hands.

Sam gawped, his mouth wide, like a goldfish going for a food pellet. 'It's cold.'

'What did having a warm heart ever do for anyone, eh? That's why you're in this situation.' Kellum prodded the heart with a stiff finger. 'No more pain, Sam. No. More. Pain.'

'No more anything,' Frank interrupted. 'You won't be able to feel. You'll be numb.'

'Pfft, caring is overrated. It just gets in the way.' Kellum waved his hands above and below the heart, 'No heartstrings either, nothing to pull on.'

Charlie entered the room carrying a tray lined with three cups of tea and a small tower of biscuits. 'I was out of order before. I'm sorr–' Charlie locked eyes with Kellum. 'What are you doing here?'

'A pleasure as always, Charlie. Not dead yet, I see?'

Charlie banged the tray down on his desk, unsettling the biscuit stack. He marched alongside Frank and looked at Sam as he gawped at the black, pulsing heart. 'You don't want to mess with that, boy. Give it back to him.'

'Nonsense, Sam. black heart is the way to go. What do these two relics know?'

'It's no good, trust me. You need to weather the storm. It's the only way to learn.' Charlie's words took on a tone that Frank hadn't heard in a while: *sincerity*.

Sam swallowed to clear his throat. 'I don't know. This could be for me. I don't want to feel the way I do now.'

'And there's no need, Sam. No need at all,' added Kellum.

Charlie began unbuttoning his shirt.

Frank looked on. 'Charlie, you don't have t–'

'No, he should see this.' Charlie's fingers worked their way down the buttons, popping them free one by one. He pulled the shirt open.

Sam gasped at what he saw. On the left side of Charlie's chest was a mass of scars that resembled congealed spaghetti. 'I had a black heart once and this is what it does to you and you don't even realise it. You can't imagine the damage it does to those around you.'

'Ew, gross,' muttered Sam.

'Shut up and listen. You'll go through life hurting everyone, not appreciating things. You won't get hurt, but you'll hurt others. Then when it's too late you'll be alone, with no one… or maybe, just maybe, you get really lucky and you meet an angel in the tackle store, and against all odds she sees a glimmer of something good, puts the time in to save you from yourself, gets rid of your black heart. But it ain't pretty and that's only if you're really lucky. I don't think there are many like my June out there.'

A slow clap echoed round reception. 'Riveting,' Kellum said feigning a yawn. He turned his attention back to Sam. 'Now, shall we discuss the details o–'

'I don't want it.'

He lobbed the heart into the briefcase. His wonder turning to disgust. 'I don't want to end up looking like that. That's fucking gross.'

'I think you're missing the point a little there, Sam. But you're making the right choice.' said Frank. Charlie buttoned up his shirt, a wry smile on his face that he pushed in Kellum's direction. He made his way back to his desk and started in on the biscuits.

'You may leave now, Kellum. I believe Sam isn't interested in what you have to offer,' said Frank.

'Sentimental idiots all of you,' Kellum hissed. He slammed the briefcase shut and dragged it off the counter. He marched towards the exit. 'Good luck with your spice rack!' he called over his shoulder before barging through the doors.

Sam turned to Frank. 'Maybe I'll try the birdhouse thing, maybe that'll help?'

'Excellent choice.' Frank gave the desk a triumphant slap and flicked through the folder.

Bang!

The main doors flew open. Frank looked up, expecting Kellum to have returned – instead, a pale young girl staggered in, her manicured hands clutching her blood-stained chest. 'I'm dying!' she wailed, as she pressed the back of her hand against her forehead.

Frank removed the birdhouse plans from the folder and pushed them across the desk to Sam. Not that he noticed, for his eyes were firmly fixed on the girl. Frank turned to a new page in the Incidents book, smoothed it over. He stood up straight and cleared his throat. 'All the way up to the counter, please, miss.'

The girl swayed left, right then staggered forward, slowly getting closer.

Ping

Ping

In perfect unison, Sam and the girl both rummaged in their pockets and pulled out mobile phones. They stared at the screens for a moment before looking up at each other. Charlie looked up from his magazine. 'What's that?' he asked, spitting crumbs.

'Dating app,' said Sam, his gaze stuck on the girl. 'Tells me when there's a seriously gorgeous single girl nearby.'

The girl smiled, a hint of colour swelling on her cheeks. 'I'm Beth.'

'I'm Sam.' Sam shot a look at his phone then back to Beth. 'Says on your bio that you like FilmFlix?'

'Uh, huh,' she beamed. 'It's one of my favourite things. Beth looked at her phone; her eyes scanned left to right. 'Says here that you like going out to eat?'

'Yeah, yeah. I really do. I love going out to eat. I ate out twice today already,' he grinned.

'Me too!' Beth gushed.

The bloodstain on Beth's top lightened and vanished leaving the crisp white cotton of her top unblemished. Sam opened his jacket and inspected his chest. The gaping hole was now covered with healthy skin. He stepped out of the tray, reached for Beth's hand and placed it on his chest.

'You fixed me.'

'And you fixed me,' Beth replied. They smiled at each other.

'Do you want to go for something to eat?'

'Yeah, I'd love to,' said Beth. They turned away from the desk and headed for the exit.

'What the... ?' spat Charlie.

Frank waved the plans in the air. 'What about the birdhouse?'

Sam looked over his shoulder.

'Birdhouse?... more like... smird mouse,' he scoffed. Beth giggled as the pair pushed through the exit and left the reception. The doors clattered shut behind them.

'And that's why you shouldn't bother,' Charlie spat, jamming another digestive in his mouth and straightening out his magazine.

'Meeeooow,' whinged Battle Cat.

'I'm getting the floor buffer out,' said Frank.

BROKEN HOME

I'm woken in the middle of the night by my old man. He must have got me pretty good because I can taste blood at the back of my throat. My eyes adjust to the dark just in time to see another fist jerk towards me and I sink my head back into my pillow to take the sting out of it. Shaking off stars, I curl into a ball and cover up, ready for another jab. Dad sways and stumbles towards the window where the orange glow from the streetlights reveal just how pathetic he looks, clothes stained with beer, a beard full of food scraps.

'Leave your Mum's stuff alone, shit for brains,' he spits, his words carried by alcohol fumes. Dad never cared about Mum when she was alive. Now she's gone, he's full of regret, and booze. *Mostly booze.* He stomps the floorboards. 'Understand?'

'Yes,' I say, sounding more afraid than I want to.

'Good. My house, my rules. Don't forget it.'

Family time over, Dad backs away and staggers out into the hallway. He slams into the bannisters, steadies himself then sways back into my room, coming so close to falling flat on his face that I'm sure he's held up by invisible strings. He lunges for the door and slams it shut so hard that it sends a lightening-strike of cracks across the wall. I hear him moving along the landing, pinballing off the bannisters and wall towards his bedroom.

'Dickhead,' I mumble.

'I hate that man,' a voice whispers.

I snap my head left and right, looking for where the words came from, wondering for a moment if Dad has finally damaged what little *'shit for brains'* I have. From the safety of my bed, I check the dark corners of my room, but there's no one there. Something splashes the back of my hand and I stifle a yell as I realise it's just the blood from my nose. 'Idiot.' I mumble, angry at myself for being scared.

It hasn't always been like this.

Dad and me haven't ever been best friends. He never took me to the park or even showed up at my birthdays, but he never hit me. All that started when Mum died. I press the edge of my sheets to my nose to try and soak up the blood, but it doesn't really help. I swing my legs out of bed, my feet touching down on the cold, rough floorboards.

'Such a terrible, horrid man,' the voice whispers again.

I retreat under the covers, wrap them around me and slam my eyes shut.

'Don't be afraid,' the voice says softly.

I lift the corner of my duvet, just high enough so I can see out. Through the dark, I can make out the outline of my chest of draws and my clothes piled messily against it. I look at the fresh cracks above the door. They look darker than the night itself. They start to reach farther across the wall and swell, like there's something behind them, trying to get through.

I shrink under the duvet keeping the peephole open, watching the cracks spit dust into the air. Long spider legs push through the gaps. They twitch and pad the wall around them before reaching towards me, floating across the room, getting closer and closer. I realise that they're not spider legs at all, but long wooden fingers jutting from a palm made of wires and bits of wool.

I slam my duvet spy-hole shut and hope my quilt is better

at soaking up piss than it is blood. 'I have something for you,' the voice says, louder, *closer*. A draft on my feet, my duvet is lifted. I try to scream but nothing comes out.

'Look. Look,' says the voice.

I peep through my fingers. At the bottom of the bed is a ball of crumpled paper. I curl up tighter and bite my lip to try and wake up, even hoping Dad will come back in and give me another punch.

'I'm not going to hurt you.'

'Please… ' I whimper.

'I have something for you.'

'I don't want it.'

'You will. Look now, please.'

The hand flicks the crumpled paper towards me. I reach out with a shaky hand and pull it in for a closer look, adjusting the cover to let more of the street-light in. I pick it apart and flatten it out. It's not just paper, it's a photo, one that I know – it's of me and Mum at the fair in front of the ghost train.

I wipe it on my chest to remove the dust and angle it towards the window for a better look. We both were so happy. I remember all the things we did that day and my smile grows so big it hurts my bloody nose. This was one of our fantastic adventures together, just Mum and me. She always called our days out *fantastic adventures.* I didn't realise just how fantastic they were until she was gone. I was a lot younger then, but I still remember everything we did that day – we got up early and went for breakfast down the greasy spoon, double sausage egg and chips, then went to the fair for the afternoon where we rode all the rides at least twice, ate hot-dogs and even won a goldfish. Dad wasn't around that day. Him and mum had argued the night before. I heard them scream at each other as I sat at the top of the stairs. They'd argue about lots of things but this time it was about money.

I remember her saying to me the next day that we should just get out for the day, leave the house for a fantastic adventure and forget about any worries we had. I was eight, I didn't have any worries, not real ones anyway. I just think she needed a fantastic adventure that day even more than I wanted one.

'Where... where did you get this?'

'It fell between the floorboards many years ago. I thought you would like it back.'

'Thanks,' I say, still smiling.

'Do you miss her?'

'Yeah,' I reply. I push the covers away and sit up.

I stare at the hand bobbing in the air. It's connected to a long, thin arm made from twisted strips of wire and splintered wood that leads back to the crack in the wall. 'I miss her too,' says the voice. 'I miss how she used to look after me and had me fixed when I needed it. She was good to us. She fixed us both, didn't she?'

'Are you... stuck in the walls?' I ask.

'I am the walls, the floors and everything else. I am this house,' the voice tells me, getting louder with each word.

'But how can you... how can a house talk?'

'How do you talk?'

'I don't know, just use my mouth, I guess.'

A tear shoots across the wall. It opens and mashes together, 'I use my mouth, too,' it explains huffing dust and curling into a smile.

'Have you always been able to talk?'

'I've never tried before.'

'So... why now?'

'I'm falling into disrepair and need your help. My floors

haven't felt carpet in years, my stairs creak, and my roof has a hole that makes my brain ache when the wind blows.'

The hand floats back across the room and slips into the cracks.

It appears moments later with a wad of wall-filling in its grasp. It hovers above me, motioning for me to take it. 'For your leaking top floor. We both need repairing before your dad demolishes us both.'

I take the fluffy wall-wool and dab it to my nose, but it just makes it itch. I put it on the bed. 'What can I do? I don't know how to fix things; I'm only fourteen.'

'I am a timeworn house and many things have been forgotten under my boards and between my bricks. All sorts of treasures. You could trade it with people, to fix me.'

'But Dad won't–'

'I could take care of him,' the House interrupts. 'There are lots of dead things in my walls. I could make him one of them.'

'Murder him?'

'*Demolish* him, so he can't hurt either of us ever again. I'm sick of him punching my walls, slamming my doors and leaking on my floors when he is drunk.'

'I'm sick of him, too. But killing him? I'm not sure.'

'Would your mother be happy if she knew how he's been treating you? She would want you to be safe. I could protect you if you'd like? We could look after each other.'

I look back at the picture of Mum and me. 'She wouldn't be happy. But I don't know if she'd want him *demolished*.'

The bedroom door creaks open. I freeze, expecting Dad to stomp in for round two.

'It's okay,' says the house. 'It's just me. Please, come down to the kitchen. I have things to show you.'

I sniff and wipe the crusty blood from my nose.

'Okay, I guess.' I kick away the covers.

*

I creep down into the kitchen. It's a mess, the worktop is covered with open packets of sandwich meat and a ripped bag of bread. Dad must have come home with the munchies. The small cracks in the wall above the fridge open and close like tiny mouths, 'Over here,' they call. I move towards them. As I get closer, the fridge begins to shake. The floorboards under it ripple like waves, lifting it up and setting it aside to reveal a faded patch of wall dusted with cobwebs.

'Watch,' say the cracks.

A small hole appears in the centre of the wall. It expands, faster and faster sending years of dust and dirt dancing into the air. I wave the dustcloud from my face. The hole slows and stops growing when it reaches the size of a dustbin lid.

'Take a look inside,' urge the cracks.

I move forward and stop just feet away. I go on tiptoes and peer into the hole. Inside, it's pitch black. 'Closer,' says the voice...

I shuffle in... *bang!* I spin round to see Dad standing in the doorway, the kitchen door shaking on its hinges. 'What the fuck are you doing to my house?!'

I try to run, but instead do an on-the-spot panic-dance without moving in any direction. Dad rushes me, his size ten sinks into my stomach, knocking me to the floor and sending my head bouncing off the boards. The room spins and I feel like I'm back at the fair on the Wurlitzer with Mum. Dad bears down on me, his hands around my neck, the booze on his breath stinging my eyes. His rough hands squeeze. 'You little prick. How dare you disrespect my house!'

The gaps in the floorboards purse together and whisper in my ear, 'Let me help you.'

'Dad… stop… please…'

His grip tightens.

'Let me help you,' they say again.

With the little breath I have, I push out the word, 'Demolish.'

The air is sucked from the room as the house takes a deep breath. The walls flex and the wooden beams that run across the kitchen ceiling break free and pull away from the plaster. They crunch and tangle together in an explosion of splinters to form a huge hand. Dad releases me and watches open-mouthed as it darts towards him. 'What the fu–' he screams, his words falling short as the fingers snap around his head and pinch him into the air.

The floorboards ripple again and carry me into the corner out of harm's way. I look up as Dad dangles like a cuddly toy caught in the grip of a fairground claw machine. Cracks race along the floor and rip open revealing a huge grin with large wooden fangs. The mouth snaps together with a deafening *crunch* sending fragments into the air. 'This is for walking shit over me,' it roars and its jaws rise over Dad's ankles…

Chomp!

Dad *screams.* The mouth chews as blood spurts from his ankles covering the wooden lips. A tongue made from boards and copper pipes flicks out over the red juice and slurps it down.

The cupboard doors swing open and the splintered hand yanks Dad towards them, his leaking ankles painting the floor red. Wires emerge from the cupboards and slither into the air like snakes. They strike, wrapping around Dad's wrists and pulling his hands inside. 'This is for wiping your dirty hands all over me,' the house screams. The doors slam and Dad's hands burst inside like balloons filled with blood.

He waves the spurting stumps at me and I lock eyes with him.

'Terry, help me,' he screams.

I point towards my aching nose. 'Sorry, Dad. I think you've hit me too hard. I can't understand what you're saying.'

Dad is yanked towards the kitchen sink and tossed into it. He lands with a meaty splat, his arms and legs spraying blood all over the worktop. The hand curls into an enormous spiked fist and pulls back across the room. 'This is for punching holes in me and your son!' It powers forward, smashing into Dad. His bones snap like twigs. The knuckles grind him into the sink to a soundtrack of *crunches* and *snaps.*

Crunch.

Snap.

Crunch.

Snap.

The fist rises, little pieces of Dad fall away and splat onto what's left of him. He twitches in my direction, his remaining eye peering out from the hunk of bloody flesh and broken bone. 'Erryyy,' he gargles and his jaw falls and dangles by a flap of skin. 'Eeeeeeryyy.'

I stifle a laugh. 'It's a very unhappy home, Dad.'

The fist hurtles forward and pounds him once more… then again, and again till he's slush and Dad trickles down the plug hole. The taps turn on, thinning him out, helping him on his way down the drain. The wooden fingers pick out what's left of him from the sink, a blood-soaked sack of punctured skin and toss him across the room towards the hole. He hits the edge with a splat and disappears inside.

The fist uncurls, its fingers settling back into the grooves on the ceiling.

The mouth presses together and stitches shut.

Moments later, the kitchen is back to normal.

I get to my feet and dust myself off.

'Over here,' the voice calls from the hole.

I move towards it. Inside, I can hear something approaching, picking up speed. 'Da.. Dad,' I mutter, knowing that there's no way he could still be alive. I move in for a better look. The wall rumbles and shakes as a burst of gold and silver spew out over the floor – coins and valuables pile up around my feet.

'I am a very old house, and I hold some very old treasures,' says the voice.

I pull a large silver plate from the pile as it keeps growing higher and higher. I give it a wipe with my hand and it shines under the kitchen lights. I look at my reflection, a huge smile creeps across my bloodied face.

*

Six years later.

I lay in bed staring up at the ceiling.

I'm in Mum and Dad's old room now. I had it redecorated and furnished just how she would have liked it, a lovely plush carpet to sink your feet into when you get out of bed, lots of beautiful furniture to organise your stuff and keep your memories safe. The rest of the house looks great, too. The windows have been fixed, new carpets everywhere and the hole in the roof has been taken care of. I'm extremely house proud, just like Mum.

I keep the photo of us both by my bedside so I can look at it and think how proud she'd be of me and of what I've done. Things are good here now, there's no more arguing, no more disrespecting the house. It's a happy home.

'Hey,' a familiar voice whispers through the darkness.

I sit up and turn on the bedside lamp.

'You okay?' I ask.

'There are people at the back door, trying to open my locks.'

I quickly snap the light off and swing my legs out of bed. My feet touch down on the cosy carpet, and I creep over to the window. I peer through the curtains and see two men wearing hoodies by the back door. One feeds a crowbar inbetween the door and the frame.

I move away from the curtains. 'Let them in,' I say.

I hear the faint *click* of a lock and footsteps downstairs.

'What shall we do with them?' the walls whisper.

'Let's give them the tour.'

SICK PUPPY

'I hate you,' I spit at Brewster, my wife's guide dog.

He stares at me, tail wagging, flicking golden hairs into the air that tumble down and settle on the living room carpet that I hoovered just yesterday. I used to like dogs, but since Janet's eyesight worsened and we got Brewster, all that has changed.

I sit up on the sofa and push the covers away. For the last eight months, this is where Janet has made me sleep. She says it's because I snore and fidget when I'm in bed with her, but I know it's to make room so Brewster can curl up next to her and get all the cuddles instead of me.

I launch my pillow at the stupid dog's face. It hits its target and falls at the mutt's feet. He sniffs it and looks back up at me, tilting his head in that dumb dog way.

'Didn't see that, did you?' I growl.

Before Brewster, my wife relied on me, I'd take her out, I'd be her eyes. I felt *needed*. Now it's all, *good boy, Brewster* and *Mummy loves you, Brewster*. He gets all the compliments, all of the affection. Wherever he goes everyone is always telling him what a *handsome boy* he is. I've never been called *handsome,* but then I guess that's because I don't have a wonderful golden coat of hair like he does. The last few hairs on my wrinkly scalp gave up the fight long ago, and over the years my head has shrunk but my nose and ears have stayed the same size.

Maybe it's good Janet can't see me.

Brewster *barks.*

I know what he's saying, I hear it clear as day. He's saying: *food now, Richard, you pathetic old man.* After his breakfast, he'll bark at me again: *Put my harness on me, you worthless piece of shit.* After that, he'll be ready to take *my* wife around town while I stay home and rot. How humiliating to be second to a dog, an animal that once, when it ate too much, spewed up and scoffed thc vomit. An animal that licks its genitals and sniffs its own shit. This dirty, filthy creature is my replacement.

I get up from the sofa and plod to the kitchen.

Brewster follows me, tail wagging, excited that he's going to have his breakfast. He sits by his bowl, expecting me to go to the fridge and prepare the steak my wife makes me buy for him.

He looks at *me,* then at the fridge.

I look at *him,* and then at the knife block.

I select a large carving knife and it makes a satisfying *snicktt* sound as I pull it free.

The time is now 7.35. Janet will wake up at 9.00, and she'll call, *Brewster come here, baby,* and he'll go running. I've not got long. Stalking towards him, he looks at the blade and barks*: What are you doing, Richard?*

I clamp my hand over his muzzle, forcing it shut.

We lock eyes and I thrust the knife up through his throat. It doesn't come out the top of his head like I expect it to, instead it gets stuck halfway up inside his skull. Brewster thrashes, I throw my weight on him and pin him to the floor, hugging him tightly. 'Not like mummy's cuddles, are they?' I whisper.

Bubbles of blood expand and *pop* around the hilt of the knife as he tries to cry out: *Mummy, help me*! I wedge the blade in deeper and rake it around inside his skull in a circular motion until finally the bubbles stop and his body falls limp.

I push him away and get to my feet to see that my shirt and trousers are saturated with blood. I know for sure this isn't going to come out in the wash. I don't mind, though, I'll have no need for clothes soon.

27 minutes 10 seconds is the exact time it takes to skin Brewster and squeeze my wrinkly naked body into his beautiful coat. Stripping Brewster of his skin was a little tricky at first, but once I got the hang of it, it was easy – like stripping a pillow of its case.

Looking in the mirror, I arrange Brewster's saggy boneless face over my own and pin it in place with the staple gun I used last year for putting up Christmas decorations. The holes where his eyes were don't exactly match up with mine, so I trim some skin away to allow me to see properly.

I look myself over. Brewster is not a perfect fit. His front paws fall a little short of covering my wrists and his belly skin is a tad tight over my own. But, I have to say, I really do look rather *handsome*.

'Brewster baby, come to mummy' Janet calls from upstairs. I grin and bound towards the sound of her voice.

Reaching the top of the stairs, I drop down on all fours and rush into the bedroom. Janet sits up in bed and pats the duvet. 'Come here, boy.' I jump up and put my paws next to her. She runs her hand over my head and through my golden coat. Her touch feels so good it makes my back leg rise and shake uncontrollably. She lifts the duvet and rubs the mattress, 'Come see Mummy.' Obeying, I leap under the quilt and settle next to her, resting my head on top of her thigh.

Being in bed with my wife, her wanting me again, makes me feel so happy. I nuzzle into her. 'Oh, Brewster, you're so cold. Let's warm you up.' Her hands move in a frantic circular motion all over me and I tremble with ecstasy. 'Do you like that, Brewster?'

I roll onto my back and expose my belly.

'Woof,' I bark.

THE BOY WITH COGS FOR A HEART

Billy, the robot boy, sat in the back of the car peering out into the night, counting the orange street lamps as they whizzed past. His human parents sat up front, in silence. Something had changed this evening, something was wrong, but he was unsure of what exactly.

Had it been something he'd done?

Had he upset Mum and Dad at the party?

Billy checked himself over to make sure all of his gears and cogs were hidden under his synthetic skin, and that he hadn't damaged himself in any way; a scuffed knee or elbow would be expensive to repair, and he knew that this would upset Mum and Dad terribly. He pushed away his thick synthetic hair on the back of his head to make sure the cover on his *off switch* wasn't up either, as this would have also have caused embarrassment – everything was intact, and you would have to look very carefully to tell that he wasn't an ordinary eight-year-old boy.

They had all been to a birthday party that evening. Mum and Dad's friends had just got a robot boy of their own. His name was Alfie, and he was the 8-year-old version just like Billy, except Alfie was the latest model and possessed more life-like traits. His skin appeared even more human, and he was able to cry like a real boy as well as being able to speak in six different languages while standing on his head. Everybody clapped and was amazed at how impressive he was, someone even hollered, 'Oh, what a delight he is!'

Billy wasn't impressed though; he thought Alfie was a snot. When the humans were out of sight, Alfie just stared at Billy like he was some form of lower life, like a toaster or trouser press. And so what if he could cry 'real' tears, Billy thought. Billy could do handstands, climb stairs three steps at a time, and swing on tree branches for hours while counting backwards – all the really *important* boy stuff.

Billy placed his hands on the backs of the car seats and pulled himself forward, poking his head between Mum and Dad.

'Look what I can do,' he said. Billy pulled his best silly face and licked his nose with the tip of his tongue. Dad kept his eyes on the road.

Mum shot a look over her shoulder. 'You've shown us that one, Billy. Sit back, please.'

Billy did as he was told.

His programming suggested the action of 'acting up' and kicking the back of Mum's seat, but Billy rejected it and opted to behave instead. A little misbehaving was encouraged by his programming to replicate a real boy, but it didn't feel right, not right now.

They all sat in silence for the remainder of the journey.

*

Back home, Billy was told to wait in the hallway while Mum and Dad went into the kitchen to discuss 'grown-up' stuff. He took a seat on the bottom stair as they shut themselves away.

Billy decided to charge himself while he waited, so he plugged himself into the socket by the stairs. The fizz of electricity buzzed in his head as his batteries slowly recharged. Sat there, his curiosity program made his mechanical insides itch like crazy. He really really wanted to know what they were talking about.

His programming stirred, suggesting a resolution. *Maybe if he got a little bit closer to the door...*

He accepted this course of action and tiptoed to the kitchen door and listened. He couldn't tell what they were saying exactly, but he was sure heard the name *Alfie*. Billy pulled away from the door and used all three-thousand and forty-eight gears in his head to scrunch his face in disgust.

Were they thinking of getting him a brother?

Billy thought how awful it would be to have a version of the snot-bag deluxe hanging around all the time, stealing attention from *his* mum and dad, and then a line of code filled his head: what mum and dad needed was something to remind them of how talented Billy was!

He unplugged himself from the wall and despite what Mum had told him to do, he ran into the kitchen. With a shout of, 'Look what I can do,' he vaulted across the table and performed a perfect somersault landing just inches away from Mum and Dad.

Billy stood, arms outstretched, awaiting the rapturous applause and praise.

Dad didn't look up. Mum barely gave a glance. 'We've seen that one, Billy,' she sighed. 'And I told you to stay out of here.'

Billy's arms dropped by his sides. He slouched from the kitchen, slamming the door behind him. He paused in the hallway. He needed something new, something they'd never seen him do. Billy scanned his database for something special, something that couldn't be ignored...

Please wait... processing...

Please wait... processing...

Please wait... processing...

He had it! He went into the downstairs toilet and turned on the sink taps, cupped water, and splashed it over his face. Billy's lack of artificial tear ducts meant he couldn't cry like snot face, but surely Mum and Dad would marvel at how inventive he was being. He left the toilet and marched towards the kitchen. Some of the water seeped into Billy's head cavity and tickled his circuits.

He paused outside the kitchen door, set his voice mode to *upset* then burst into the kitchen. He marched directly in front of Mum and Dad and began wailing – 'But... but... but–'

'Go to bed, Billy!' Mum snapped. She composed herself, then spoke again, softer this time, 'Go upstairs, Billy, and I'll be up in a bit to read you a story.'

Billy beamed. The words were music to his central processor; Billy loved hearing stories. He pushed Alfie to the back of his hard drive, bolted from the kitchen and raced up the stairs (three at a time).

*

Billy flew into his bedroom and slid under the covers of his cowboy print duvet. Blankets were not a necessity when you were a robot boy as robots didn't get cold, but Billy loved the gunslinger print on the front, and he wanted to be the best robot boy he could, by doing all the things real boys did.

He pulled the covers up to his chin and waited.

Eventually, Mum and Dad appeared in the bedroom doorway. Dad leant against the frame. Mum moved around him and came and sat by Billy. She smiled and began stroking his synthetic hair from front to back. Billy opened his mouth, 'Can yo–'

'Shhhh,' Mum replied. But Billy couldn't *shhh,* he was

bursting to tell Mum and Dad just how he felt, 'I know I'm not as good as Alfie, but I love you and Dad so much. I'll be the best robot boy ever. I promise,' he beamed.

Mum leant forward and kissed his cheek. Her fingers crept spider-like round the back of his head.

'What are you doing, Mu–' Billy's words fell short, he realised... *Mum was going for his off switch!*

'No, Mum, please!'

Before he could get another word out, Mum flicked the switch. Billy's voice box was robbed of power and only the sound of whirls and clicks left his mouth. His body was shutting down. He tried to reach for her hands, maybe he could play patty cake with her to change her mind but his mechanical limbs felt like quicksand as the last spark of power was sucked from them.

'I'm sorry, Billy.'

Billy's body went rigid and locked-out, his face frozen in a look of terror, capturing his last artificial emotion perfectly.

*

The next day Mum and Dad were back to normal, in fact they were brimming with excitement. Their front room was a hive of activity as engineers from the robot company demoed their new robot boy. It was the same version as Alfie, but Mum and Dad had named it Simon.

Mum and Dad laughed and hugged each other and were so happy with the new arrival. Simon was singing pop songs in French when a fat engineer walked down the stairs carrying Billy's little body under his arm like dirty washing. Mum managed to peel herself away from all the fun for a moment to speak to the engineer.

'What will happen to him?'

'We'll strip him down and use the parts for something new.'

'Oh, that's good to know. We always recycle in this house.'

With a nod, the engineer made his way out of the house to the driveway. He yanked open the back doors of a large white van and hurled Billy inside. Billy's body crashed onto a heap of other robot children, displacing them about the floor of the van. Although they were different models, they all had the same horrified look, frozen on their faces.

The engineer slammed the doors shut.

Lying there, in the dark, in a twisted heap, the water that was trapped in Billy's head cavity seeped from his eye and ran down his cheek.

If you didn't know any better you'd think he was crying.

TOILET

'There's someone in the toilet.'

I'm pulled from sleep, expecting to see my boy in the doorway in his pyjamas, looking scared, about to tell me he's had a bad dream. Instead, my wife darts under the covers, breaking the seal and letting in the cold.

'What are you doing?'

'There's someone in the toilet,' she whispers.

I lift my head from the pillow. 'It's just Bobby. He's prob–'

'Shhh.' Kelly's cold fingers clamp my arm. 'No. *In* the toilet... at the bottom of it.'

Kelly tells me that she got up to take a piss. When she was done, she wiped herself and went to toss the tissue in the bowl. It was then that she saw it – at the bottom of the toilet, the face of an old man, his eyes looking up at her through a swirling cloud of urine, the tip of his nose just breaking the water's surface.

Then he winked at her.

'You imagined it.'

'No. He's in there. James, please.'

I kick my legs out of bed.

'I'm telling you, there's a man in the toilet,' Kelly whispers through a crack in the duvet.

I shuffle along the landing towards the bathroom door. The light from inside frames its edges, lifting it from the dark. I pass Bobby's bedroom to see his duvet peeled back, his bed empty.

I knock on the bathroom door. It creeps forward, and I push on it, 'Bobby, your mum–'

Then *I* see it.

Not a face, but legs, two legs sticking up from the toilet bowl, kicking wildly, soles slapping against the cistern.

Not a man's legs, but a boy's.

I race in and grab Bobby's ankles, lifting as hard as I can. He's pulled lower, the rim of the toilet at his knees. I fight for control, and something gives – I'm falling, the floor rushes to meet me, and blood from Bobby's severed limbs spray the ceiling. My head smacks against the tiles, and for a moment I'm still holding the legs as they kick and jerk in my hands, trying to get away.

Kelly screams.

Looking back, I see her collapse against the door frame and gather on the floor as if her bones have turned to mush. I move towards the toilet, smearing blood over the tiles with my hands and knees. Sticking my head over the bowl, I peer inside. At the bottom, below the crimson water, the face of an old man looks up at me. We lock eyes, and a smile presses his cheeks against the bowl.

Then with a *wink*, he's gone.

A GOOD WIFE

I admire the dining table. The beautiful candles, the hand-woven table cloth John and I got for our wedding, the silver cutlery arranged around a stunning bouquet of roses and lilies as the centrepiece. Everything is laid out with military precision and polished to perfection – a beautiful spread. As good a scene as any to end eight years of marriage.

At the head of the table, slumped over in a pool of drool, is handsome John Myer. My John Myer. I look at my husband and wonder for a moment when he decided that what we had wasn't enough. When I wasn't enough, and why he turned to cheating on me. I can't say it's all been bad for there was a time when I'd do anything for that man. To be honest, part of me still would.

I bang the plate of fricasseed meat and steamed vegetables down on the table, loud enough to wake the sleeping cheat. He stirs and lifts his head, strings of drool clinging to the expensive tablecloth. He wipes his mouth and shakes his head like a man shaking off a punch to the face. Now, at this moment, John doesn't look that handsome to me anymore, in fact, he looks ugly – I'd very much like to punch that face.

John Myer speaks. 'Sorry, honey. Fell asleep.'

He adjusts himself and straightens up.

He scans the plate of food and snatches up the knife and fork. He cuts the meat and shovels it in his big cheating mouth, chewing mechanically.

Chew.

Chew.

Chew.

I take the seat at the opposite end of the table, pull a silver ring from a napkin, lay it over my lap and take a *small* sip of wine. I don't want to drink too much. I want to be able to appreciate the look on John's face when I tell him I know about his sordid little affair. My mind turns to Susan, the other woman, the younger, tauter version of myself. I won't kid myself and say I don't know what he sees in her for she is beautiful – which makes me wonder: if I had gone to the gym more, and did a gazillion crunches and ate nothing but rabbit food, would he have strayed? *But of course he would, that's what dogs do.*

'I feel really tired,' John spits.

He cumbersomely attacks his plate of food with all the grace of a caveman.

'Well, you've been working hard lately. All those *late* nights' — the words come out louder than I expect and they sound more than a little accusatory. I had wanted to wait until after our meal for the big reveal, the twist in the tale, but it seems I may struggle.

I wait for him to ask: *what is the matter? I can tell something's up, baby.* But he keeps scoffing, chewing.

Chew.

Chew.

Chew.

I take a deep breath. Here goes. 'I know –'

'You have a mark, on your neck,' John interrupts, knocking the wind from my sails. He prods his own neck as if I'm confused and need further indication where he means when he says 'neck'. He turns his attention back to his food, keeps shovelling.

I swivel in my chair and look back to the mirror, and sure

enough, a smudge of burgundy on my neck. *This won't do.* I want everything to be perfect for our meal.

'Work was hectic. The emergency room was packed today,' I say, and I dip my napkin into a glass of water and wipe at the offending mark.

John motions to his plate of food with his fork, 'Needs salt,' he informs me. It doesn't need salt, but as John has proven, he has terrible taste. Ever the dutiful wife I stand, an old mechanism inside me that still somehow wants to please.

'I'll get it,' I say. I fold my napkin from my lap and set it next to my plate. I leave the room.

In the kitchen, the worktop resembles one of the operating tables at the hospital with all the blood splatter and medical equipment scattered about. I scan the mess and wonder when this is over, will I do the washing up and tidy or just call the police?

No, no need to let myself down.

I'll do the washing up, clean as I usually would, *then* call the police.

I spy the salt among the syringes that I borrowed from work.

I pick it up and peer around the corner back into the dining room.

John Myer is still chewing and dribbling like a dog – the drugs are doing their thing, being reliable, unlike John.

I walk back into the room and salt John's meat for him before resuming my place at the table. I take another sip of the wine and decide now is the time.

'I know about Susan.'

I sit back and wait for him to squirm, to reel in horror. He barely flinches.

'Who?' he mumbles.

Did I overdo it with the drugs? My words aren't carrying any weight. He needs to be confronted with evidence… that will get his attention. I reach into my pocket and place a mobile phone on the table.

His eyes widen in recognition. 'What's that?'

'It's your old phone, John. The one you thought you lost. I have found it for you.'

John tries to snatch it but moves like he's underwater. I remove it from his reach.

'It's not where it looks like,' he slurs.

I tap the phone and a picture of Susan, half-naked, showing that incredible figure, fills the screen.

'What's that?' John asks, unconvincingly, barely able to look at it. 'Just the boys at work, messing around,' he adds. No Oscar nomination for him, he's a terrible liar.

'Really? Well, let's see what you and the boys have been texting.' Instinctively I click on the text. I know what it says by heart, I've read it a thousand times, but it's too good a prop just to let it sit there.

I stand, straighten up, clear my throat and read on, 'You look amazing. I can't wait to eat your pussy.' I place the phone down, and glare at John. 'It's not very Mills and Boone, is it my dear?'

'It's not what you think.'

Is this the default vocabulary when a man is caught cheating?

It's not what you think – It's not what it looks like – It was a mistake.

I had wished for something more original, but then this is *my* John Myer we're talking about. John Myer who gave up eight years of marriage for a tighter hole to stick his *thing* in.

His big floppy mouth opens again to spew drivel. 'I –'

I shut him down: this is my moment. 'I've done everything for you. For the last eight years, I've been there for support,

I've cooked, I've cleaned, I've even let you do that sex thing to me that you know I can't stand and you've tossed me aside like last week's crossword.'

John tries to get up, but the drugs have him – he crashes back into his chair.

I hurry to the kitchen, eager for the finale.

I return, pushing a wheelchair containing a beautiful blonde: Susan. Her head hanging low, unconscious, another of my fine tablecloths covering her lower body.

Another thing she's ruined, *the cow*.

'What have… you… done?' slurs John.

'As always, John. I've done my duty as your wife and given you what you wanted.' And with that line delivered, I take the edges of the tablecloth and whip it away from Susan to reveal her naked body. Her inner thighs are caked with blood, a cavernous, red, slick hole exposing the bones of her pelvis where that penis-hugging vagina once was.

Dribble pours from John's lips as he releases a low whine, sounding like the dog he is. I take the phone from the table, straighten up and clear my throat, and read the text once more. 'I really want to eat your pussy.' I look at John's empty plate and shoot him a smile.

'So tell me, John. How did it taste?'

THE NIGHT BUS

Becky sat at the bus stop munching a burger. Some orange burger-juice fled the bun and slopped down her top. 'Oh, fuck it.'

'Bus will be here in a minute,' Emma said looking up from her phone.

Becky licked her fingers, wiped the mark and made it worse. 'Oh, drop me out,' she muttered.

The night bus strained over the hill like a harbinger of hope. Emma got that feeling that comes from having your ride home in sight after spending a week's wage in a London club and waiting in the cold for forty minutes.

Becky pushed herself up and made an unsteady trek to the bin where she slam-dunked the remainder of her burger. 'Gym tomorrow.'

'I don't think you'll be doing anything tomorrow, Becks. Come on, let's get you home,' said Emma, sounding more like Becky's mum than her best friend.

The bus squealed to a halt beside them, the doors clattered open.

'I love you, Em,' said Becky, blasting Emma with alcohol fumes.

'I know. I know.'

This dynamic was par for the course on a night out in the city. Becky always drank too much, and Emma was designated level-headed and sometimes *boring cow*. It was a role Emma played well. Becky got on the bus with all the grace of a baby wearing flip-flops. Emma followed, closely, making sure she didn't eat the floor. The driver, an old man with a weathered face and a grey nicotine-ravaged beard, grinned. 'Evening, girls. Disappointing night, eh?'

'What?' said Becky, projecting the word like a swear as she tapped her Oyster card on the reader.

'No fellas with you. Going home alone,' he said as his gaze lingered at the burger sauce on Becky's top. 'You got a little "special sauce" on you there, luv.'

Becky's face scrunched, 'Go fu–'. Emma shoved her along inside the bus and tapped her card on the reader. She shot the driver a fake smile and followed her intoxicated friend.

'Mouthing off is not going to get us home, Becks.'

'Creepy fucker,' Becky called back as she swung around the handrail and headed up to the top deck.

The doors clattered shut, and the bus pulled away.

Emma caught up with Becky halfway up the stairs, using a combination of wall and handrail to make her ascent. The smell of the top deck hit her with an aroma of rotten food marinated in piss. Most of the seats were taken by the usual suspects: a guy who had 'fingered some sort in the club toilet' and struggled with volume control. Girls proclaiming 'Stacy is a slag and she's gonna get it', and a few passengers who had slammed way too many shots and missed their stops.

Emma ushered Becky around legs that littered the aisle and the odd rolling beer-can into a seat near the back of the bus. Emma shuffled into a seat behind her. She hunched over, popped off her high-heels. Wiggling her toes felt like heaven. Becky fidgeted in front, trying to get comfortable. She rested her head against the window. 'They should give you pillows on the night bus.'

'Sit next to me and put your head on my shoulder if you

want.' Becky pulled herself up and fell into the seat next to Emma. She nuzzled into her. 'I love you, Em.'

'I know, you told me. Shut up now. I'm putting my headphones in.'

Becky grinned and shut her eyes.

Emma fished her phone and headphones from her pocket. She jammed them in her ears and tapped the phone's screen. Music filled her head and drowned out the background chatter. She closed her eyes…

When she opened them, she was cold, and the bus was dark and still. She looked around to see she was alone. Emma pulled out her headphones. 'Hello?' she called. The word sounded like thunder in the silence. She pushed her nose against the window and peered out. It was even darker outside, no moonlight, no stars, just twisted grey shapes set against pure black. Emma checked her phone. She thumbed the screen and was met with the 'charge battery' icon.

Emma reached down and picked up her heels. She got up and felt her way along the seats towards the stairwell. She skimmed an empty can with her foot. It scuttled across the floor and rattled down the steps. Emma winced as each step the can hit sent a loud clatter through the bus. She grabbed the handrail and made her way to the lower deck. 'Hello,' she called again, already knowing that there would be no answer.

There was nothing on the lower deck but a scattering of trash left by clubbers and partiers. Emma checked the doors, only to find them shut tight. She reached above them, and her fingers found the handle of the emergency release mechanism. She yanked it back, and the doors strained open.

The smell of petrol stung Emma's nose. She stepped out, placed a bare foot on cold concrete and looked around, her eyes adjusting to pluck out the shapes of cars and vans from the darkness.

Some sort of garage.

Her eyes were drawn to light shimmering across the glass of a large window on the far side of the room. Emma ran her hands over the soles of her feet to free pieces of grit from her skin. She slipped her shoes on and headed towards the light, feeling her way through the darkness, edging forward slowly, trying not to trip over anything.

'Alright, there?' Torchlight dazzled Emma. She jumped bringing her arms across her chest.

'Easy, luv. It's alright.'

Emma's eyes focused, and she recognised the man as the bus driver.

'I thought I heard someone poking around out here,' he said.

'Where am I?'

'At the bus garage.'

Emma took a deep breath. Her heart settled into her chest. 'I fell asleep on the bus. You should have checked there was no one there.'

'I didn't see you up there.'

'I was with my friend, Becky. Did you see her get off?'

'A lot of people get off my night bus.'

'Dark hair, pretty,' Emma offered. 'Burger-sauce girl.'

'Nah, don't remember her. She sounds tasty, though,' the bus driver grinned.

Emma offered a pretend smile. 'Please, can I use your phone? Mine's dead.'

'You'll have to use the line in the office. No mobile signal here. It's because of all the metal, I reckon. Follow me.' The man pointed his torch towards the light from the window. The beam glided over a graveyard of old cars and vans showing this place to be more scrap yard than garage. He led Emma past an old beaten-up caravan with grime covered windows.

'Not many busses in here for a bus garage,' she said.

'The main depot gets chock-a-block from time to time, so I do some repairs on the side here. Don't dob me in though, will ya? Not exactly company approved.'

'I won't,' said Emma. 'I just want to go home.'

'Good girl.'

They reached the office. The bus driver held the door open. 'After you, luv.' Emma smiled and entered. The smell of stale tobacco hung in the air and leached the moisture from Emma's throat. She looked around at the clutter covering the desk and the various objects and oddments packed onto bowing shelves.

'It doubles as the lost and found,' said the bus driver turning off his torch and setting it down on his desk next to an ashtray overflowing with roll-up fag-ends. Emma's gaze snagged on a calendar hung crookedly on the wall – a naked woman with huge breasts spraying herself with a garden hose.

'That's embarrassing,' said the driver as he waded through rubbish to get to it. 'Don't really get many birds back here.' He grabbed the top of the calendar and flipped it down, the topless picture now hidden by an even more graphic photo of a woman grasping an erect cock, her lips eager to meet it. The driver turned to Emma as if he hadn't noticed. 'There,' he smiled. 'Now let's sort you out.' He placed his hands on Emma's shoulders and ushered her aside, moving behind her and shutting the door. 'You cold?' he said, switching on an electric heater that blasted out hot tobacco air.

'If I can just use your phone, I'll get out of here.'

The bus driver slumped in the chair at the side of his desk

and rooted around in his trouser pocket. He pulled out a pouch of tobacco. 'Don't you wanna have a smoke first?'

'No, just the phone, please.'

The driver pulled open one of the desk drawers. Inside it was crammed with lighters and crumpled fag packets. Amongst them were little bags containing pills and the remnants of white powder. 'You sure? I got everything here. It's amazing what gets left behind on my night bus.' He rummaged inside, flicking empty fag packs over the floor and pulled out a plastic strip containing four blue tablets. 'I think these' uns are Viagra.' He held them up and shook them at Emma. 'Make a man rock solid, these will.'

'Are you going to let me use your phone or not?' Emma asked, her voice cracking.

The bus driver sat forward, took keys from his jacket pocket, and placed them on the desk. 'Getting hot in here,' he said shrugging his jacket from his shoulders. Emma locked eyes on specks of blood on his white shirt and an unmistakable orange stain rubbed into the cotton of his top.

'Burger sauce,' Emma whispered. Her heart boomed, and her guts did somersaults.

The bus driver looked himself over to see what had Emma so uneasy. 'Ha, oh bollocks,' he said flicking a yellow tongue over his thumb and rubbing the stain. He pushed himself up. 'I was gonna romance you first. Guess we'll just get to the lovin'.' The bus driver lunged at Emma, his hands reaching for her neck. Emma threw a punch into the old man's face, sending him crashing backwards. She snatched the keys from the desk and darted out into the darkness of the warehouse.

Struggling to see, she turned and looked back through the office window at the torch she'd left on the bus driver's desk.

The bus driver got to his feet, cupping his bleeding nose in his hands. 'Fucking bitch!'

Emma ran, slamming into cars and stumbling over objects hidden by the dark. She reached down without breaking her stride and yanked the shoes from her feet. She tossed them over her shoulder and poured on the speed. Behind her, she heard the door to the office slam shut, the light of the driver's torch scanning the garage trying to pinpoint her. She ducked behind a car and fought to catch her breath.

'I'm gonna give you a great night, luv. You went out looking for a boy, you found yourself a man!' called the driver. 'I've popped two of them blueys just for you.'

Emma set off on her hands and knees, creeping along the floor. Her hand pressed down on something – a broom handle zipped through the air and fell next to her. The torchlight jerked in her direction. She threw herself up and clambered through the side door of the old caravan. She shut the door behind her and backed inside. The floor felt crusty and rough on the soles of her feet as she shuffled along, padding around in the dark for something to use as a weapon. Emma's fingers curled around a lighter. She dropped low to the floor and flicked the wheel. A spark turned to a flame and threw a dull light on her surroundings. She scanned the rubbish-littered floor, passing the lighter over old cans and food packets – she froze when the flame illuminated a pair of bare feet amongst the mess. Emma looked up to see Becky, her hands tied above her head and secured to the roof, a rag stuffed in her mouth.

Becky jerked. 'Hhhhm!'

'Becks?' Emma leapt up and pulled the filthy cloth from her mouth.

'Em?' Becky spluttered.

'Yes. It's me.' Emma wiped Becky's bloody brow with shaking hands. 'Are you okay?'

'Yeah, I think so. He said he was going back for you–'

'He's looking for me. I've got his keys. I'll get us out of here, but we need to be quiet.' Emma pocketed the lighter and fumbled with Becky's restraints, unsure how effective she was being.

With a bang, the door swung open. Light invaded the space and rested on Becky's bloodied face. The bus driver stalked towards her. 'Your friend's got me all worked up. Not sure who I'm gonna romance first. I'm gonna fi–'

Emma leapt from the darkness and hurled herself at the bus driver. The man turned and struck her with the torch, sending her crashing into the sea of rubbish. 'Leave her alone!' Becky screamed, drawing his attention. Emma shook off the blow and pushed herself up. 'Emma, run!'

Emma threw herself through the open door. The bus driver reached for her snatching only air. She raced away, weaving through the garage, the concrete floor cutting and mangling the soles of her feet. Eventually, she found herself back at the bus. She darted inside, ricocheting off the wall and landing next to the driver's cubicle. Emma dragged herself up and fought to open the driver's compartment.

'Driver's only beyond this point, darling.' The bus driver stood in the aisle, his flashlight shining in Emma's eyes. He stomped towards her and grabbed a handful of her hair. Emma fought back, but a blow from the butt of the torch sent her spinning to the floor. The bus driver loomed over her. 'You're feisty aint yah? Bet I can learn that out of you.' Emma struggled to get up, her head was spinning, she felt like she was at the centre of a tornado. The driver fell on top of her and pinned her to the floor. He sunk a fist into her face and began unbuckling his belt. 'I loves me a city girl.'

'We're from out of town, fuck face.'

The bus driver looked over his shoulder to see Becky bring a wrench down on his head. The impact rattled through his skull and sent his teeth pinging off the windows of the lower deck. Becky grabbed his collar and dragged him from Emma. She hit him again, sending an almighty CRACK echoing through the bus. She struck again and again, not stopping until the driver's head was nothing but a mess of skull and well-beaten brains. Blood flowed, filling the grooves in the floor and seeping along the aisle of the bus.

Becky dropped the wrench and helped Emma stand. 'You okay?'

Emma threw her arms around Becky; the two hugged each other as tight as they could. 'I love you,' said Emma.

'I know, I know,' said Becky.

Emma looked over Becky's shoulder at the driver's dead body. 'What do we do now?' she asked.

Becky stepped back and thumbed the tears away from Emma's cheeks.

'Get a fucking cab.'

#MEGALOLZ

Tanya gazed at her reflection in the toothpaste-flecked bathroom mirror. She admired her bronzed body achieved by spending the summer on the beach #GoldenGoddess, then turned and checked out her firm butt earned by spending the summer nights at the gym #HottiesWhoLift. The new underwear from John looked amazing hugging her curves and she thought it was only right to let him compliment her and beg for a pic of what was underneath #BoysTotheYard.

Tanya's flatmate was out getting wined, dined and worshipped by some rich banker, so she had the place to herself – *time for some fun!* – she snatched her mobile from the side of the sink and pushed away tampons, balls of used dental floss and anything else that could ruin #SelfiePerfection.

With the phone pointed at the mirror, she tilted her pelvis and twisted her body to just the right angle to make her boobs go from *good* to *OMG*! She then ruffled her long black hair to add volume #TotallyNaturalMane and pulled the perfect duck face.

She tapped the screen – *click* – it was a sound that never failed to get her excited as it always meant compliments and adoration would soon follow: #SoooPretty. #TenOutofTen.

She checked the image – *amazing* – as always. Sure, you could see the toilet in the background and the unmade bed through the gap in the door, but who would care about that? #YouJustJelly.

She sent the pic to John and waited. The thought of getting him hot and bothered made her feel good. Maybe she'd send him another, showing more flesh, and whip him into a total frenzy #LikeABoss. The thought of this caused a warmth to rush between Tanya's legs. It started to intensify and her mind turned to #SelfLove...

PING – a reply from John.

She snatched up the phone, ready for praise – she tapped the screen, the message snapped across the display: *Who the fuck is that behind you in the pic!?* Tanya spun around and was met with the slash of a blade across her face #LeaveANastyScar.

She stumbled back and smashed her head on the toilet as she crashed to the floor.

Her attacker #MaskedIntruder loomed over her with a #BigFuckingKnife. He pulled a phone from his pocket and dragged Tanya up by her hair. She thrashed as he pulled her closer and forced her face next to his. Angling his phone at the mirror, he tapped the screen – *click* – and started to type. He forced Tanya to look at the deranged selfie, its heading... #BodyNeverFound #MegaLolz.

THE HANDYMAN

'Okay, let's see what we've got.'

The handyman pulls a retractable knife from his tool bag. He extends the blade and presses it into the crisp tape of the cardboard packaging with a satisfying *pop*. He draws the blade along the seal. The lid bobs open.

Young Tommy watches from the doorway.

Handyman slides his hands inside the box and pulls out two large white panels that he places flat on the floor, side by side. He delves again and removes two smaller, medium-sized panels that he places next to the larger panels. He goes back in again and again, reaching deeper each time.

Moments later, the front room carpet is covered in panels and boards of different shapes and sizes, all neatly arranged and spaced with military precision.

Tommy watches.

Handyman fishes out a plastic packet filled with screws and fittings. He lays it on the floor and jabs it with the knife. He splits it open, spreading its contents over the carpet. He separates, screws, cam locks, cam dowels and other fixings into neat piles.

He pulls his tool bag to his side and removes a worn claw-hammer.

Tommy watches.

'Tommy, out the way.' Grace, Tommy's mother, enters the room. She places her hand on the little boy's chest and ushers him out into the hallway. 'How long will this take?'

Handyman turns away from his perfectly arranged pieces. 'Hour maybe?'

'Well, just quick as you can, please. I've got lots to do.' Grace marches off.

Tommy resumes his spot. Handyman smiles at him. 'You the foreman today?' Tommy ignores the question; instead, he offers up a silver cowboy gun.

'Have you seen my gun?'

'Wow, that's good, mate. You're not gonna shoot me are you?'

Tommy considers. 'Are you a baddie?'

Handyman reaches for his hammer; he tosses it up in the air and it spins twice before landing perfectly in the palm of his hand. 'Nah, I'm a goodie,' he grins.

Tommy chuckles. 'Ha, that's really cool.'

Handyman turns back to his work. He selects a large panel from the row and picks up a handful of wooden dowels from the pile. He inserts the wooden dowels into pre-drilled holes, then with a succession of fast, hard hits with the hammer, he bang, bang, bangs them into place.

'My dad's got one of those,' says Tommy.

Handyman rests the hammer on the carpet. 'Has he now?' He picks up his knife and extends the blade. 'Has he got one of these too?'

'I think so. Daddy says th… but I'm not allowed… I'm not allowed to touch it.'

'Your old man's right. It's real sharp.'

Grace looms in the doorway. 'Tommy, stop distracting the man,' she says, her voice unpleasant and shrill. Handyman retracts the blade, lays the knife with the hammer.

Tommy protests, 'But I was just telling–'

'Shut up, Tommy. You're giving me a headache. Pick a

film to watch or something.' Grace points to poorly stacked DVDs next to the TV.

'I've watched all those.' Tommy flicks an arm in the direction of a shelf up high loaded with neatly arranged DVDs. 'Can I watch one of Daddy's films?'

'No, Tommy. Stop asking,' Grace spits. 'They'll give you nightmares.'

Handyman selects a medium-sized panel.

Grace continues, 'I swear you do this on purpose.'

Handyman pulls more wooden dowels from the pile, jams them into the predrilled holes of the medium panel. Selects his hammer.

Grace still isn't finished, 'I'm telling yo–'

BANG, BANG, BANG Handyman whacks the dowels into place.

Grace glares at him. 'Do you–'

'Tea would be nice,' says Handyman.

'What?'

'Tea. Two sugars. Milky.'

Grace ponders the request, considering it a massive inconvenience.

'Please,' adds Handyman.

Grace leaves the room, muttering as she goes.

Tommy moves back into position.

Handyman continues his work. He delves into his tool bag and removes a Phillips screwdriver. He selects three cam locks from the pile and drops them into place on the surface of the large panel. He then selects three cam dowels from another pile and begins screwing them into the face of the medium-sized panel. With four and a half twists, the first cam dowel sits neatly and securely in place. Handyman looks over at Tommy who is busy treading on his own feet and swaying against the door frame.

'What aintya allowed to watch, mate?' Handyman asks.

Tommy lifts his head and points towards the forbidden shelf. 'Daddy's films, they say I get nightmares, but I won't.'

Handyman places his screwdriver down and gets to his feet. He steps carefully around his well-arranged pieces and plucks a DVD from the shelf. He scans the cover for a moment before flipping it over and examining the back. 'Nah, this is alright. I let my kids watch this one all the time. They don't get nightmares.' Handyman holds the DVD towards Tommy. 'You want this one?'

Tommy nods.

Handyman navigates to the TV. He kneels down and taps the 'eject' button on the DVD player. The tray strains open. He cracks open the DVD case and spears the disc with a stiff finger.

'Excuse me. What the hell do you think you're doing?' Grace stands in the doorway. She drags Tommy away and deposits him in the hall.

Handyman rises and points his finger at Grace, waggling the DVD on the tip. 'I was putting this on for the little man.'

'He's not allowed to watch that.' Grace wades in with no respect for the perfect arrangement of parts adorning the carpet. Her first careless step knocks the cam lock pile into the wooden dowel pile which then spills into the cam dowel pile. Her second sends the medium panels askew throwing the line into disarray. She snatches the DVD from Handyman's wiggling finger. 'Did you not hear what I told him?' She snaps it back in its case and waves it in his face. 'This isn't child appropriate.'

'I didn't know. It ain't that bad, my kids lov–.'

'I'll thank you not to interfere, please!' Grace stalks towards Tommy, knocking more pieces out of line. 'Christ, does it need to be spread out like this?' At the door, she grabs the boy by his arm. He stands on tippy toes to stop himself from dangling. Grace looks over her shoulder. 'Can you just do what you're here for, please. I'm very busy today.' She storms off, dragging Tommy behind.

Handyman surveys the disorder. He kneels down and resets his piles of fittings, pushing everything back where it should be. He realigns the panels so they are uniform once more. He plucks three cam locks from the pile and drops them into pre-drilled holes on the surface of the large panel.

Grace's lambasting of Tommy continues in the kitchen. *'I've had enough today,' she screeches.*

'I didn't do anything,' Tommy pleads.

Handyman continues his work.

He leans the large panel on its side and offers up the medium panel next to it, making sure the cam locks line up with the cam dowels and that the wooden dowels are in line with the pre-drilled holes. He adds a small amount of wood glue to the tips of the wooden dowels, then with a push and a wiggle he slots the panels together. He retrieves a slotted screwdriver from his bag and uses it to tighten the cam locks. With a half-turn to the right on each lock, the panels draw securely together.

'But I didn't do anything, Mummy.'

Handyman selects a small panel and two wooden dowels.

'That's it,' shouts Grace. Tommy's cries follow the sound of a hard thump.

Handyman pauses.

'But... I just wanted...'

'Shut up, Tommy! Shut up!'

Handyman places the two wooden dowels back on the pile and sets the small panel back down. He returns his slotted screwdriver to his tool bag. He picks up the Philips screwdriver and sets that inside as well.

'... to watch Daddy's film.'

'For Christ sake, shut up!'

Handyman retrieves his hammer and knife and puts them into his tool bag. He gathers the handles of the bag and leaves the room.

In the kitchen, Grace kneels in front of Tommy, shaking him by his shoulders. 'You're going to bed early. I'm sick of all this nonsense all the time.' Handyman drops his heavy bag onto the polished floor tiles.

Grace's head snaps. 'Can I help you?'

'Is that tea ready? I'm parched.'

'For crying out loud,' mutters Grace. She stomps over to a kettle on the worktop. She pulls sugar and teabags from the cupboards and begrudgingly gets on with it. Tommy rubs a clumsy backhand over his teary eyes. Handyman shoots him a wink.

Grace dumps two sugars into the tea and hands it over. 'Here.'

'Much obliged.'

'Right, you've got your tea. Now please just go in there and do your job.'

Handyman lifts the cup to his lips, slurps.

He lowers it. 'Eurgh, that's just awful.'

'What did you say?'

He stares at Grace. 'I said it tastes awful.'

'You– '

Handyman slams the mug to the floor; it smashes sending pieces scuttling in all directions. Grace jolts back. 'Get out. I want you out.' Her voice is no longer shrill and loud, but shaky and weak.

Handyman reaches into his bag, selects his claw-hammer.

Grace scuttles back. 'Please, just go,' she begs. She snatches at Tommy's shirt, trying to pull him close; he breaks for the kitchen table and slides under, tangling himself amongst the chairs. 'Run Tommy!' Grace shouts, scrambling behind the breakfast bar.

Handyman drops to one knee. He looks at the boy hiding amongst the chair legs. 'You being foreman, mate?' Tommy doesn't reply. 'Good man.'

Grace clumsily pulls the phone from the wall. Handyman hurls his hammer at her head. It connects with a meaty *thwack* sending a bright spray of red over the crisp white units.

Grace collapses.

Handyman moves in. He stands over her twitching body slumped against the kitchen units. 'Huuurr neer,' she dribbles and bleeds, struggling to operate her arms.

Handyman retrieves his hammer. Kneels at her side, 'You're a terrible parent. You just scream and shout at the boy. What's worse, you leave him in a room with a stranger. A total stranger. I could be anybody... I could be a very bad man.' Handyman rises. He tosses his hammer in the air. It spins twice before landing perfectly in the palm of his hand. 'Lucky for you I'm a decent bloke.'

Tommy peaks around the counter. He looks at his blood covered mother.

'I'm a goodie, aint I, mate?' Handyman asks him.

'You, you did that,' Tommy says.

'It was an accident, mate. She was supposed to catch it. Bet you would of caught it, wouldn't yah?'

Tommy nods. Grace's body shakes and thrashes. Handyman steps back. 'That's never happened before,' he says.

'What's, what's wrong with mummy?' asks Tommy.

'She's broken, mate.'

'Broken?'

'Yeah. Shall we open her, see what's wrong?'

Tommy nods.

'Right you are, little man.' Handyman moves past the boy and pushes the kitchen table to the back of the room. He stacks chairs on top of each other and makes a large space in the centre. He walks back to Grace, grabs her ankles and drags her into the middle.

'We need a lot of space, mate, so we can see all the parts laid out.'

Tommy nods.

'Good lad. You're not the foreman anymore. You're gonna be my apprentice. First job, pass me my tool bag.' The young boy grabs the handles of the bag and drags it to Handyman. He delves inside, pulls out a retractable knife, and looks Grace over. 'Okay, let's see what we've got.'

Young Tommy watches.

THE LITTLE SHOP OF REVENGE

I traipse along the high street with my hand over my cheek, partly in an attempt to ease the ache from the face slap, but mostly to hide what John Peaceman and his gang drew on me when they jumped me after school.

Stopping outside the sweetshop, I wipe away tears and check my reflection in the window. On my cheek, in black marker, is a crudely-drawn spunking cock. 'How many times?' I whine. Last time, John drew a pair of tits across my face, and the time before that he drew a vagina on my nose. By the end of the year I'm going to be the marker pen equivalent of a Picasso.

'Hey, Billy!'

I turn to see Simon rushing towards me.

'I was running and calling after you, then this car almost hit me, but I styled it out and rolled over the bonnet. I was like, learn to drive, you mug,' he tells me with great enthusiasm. Simon's mum worked in the paint factory when she was pregnant with him, and I think he soaked up a lot of the fumes and they damaged the part of his brain that separates fantasy from reality. At school, it's earned him the nickname Chat-Shit-Simon.

'Didn't hear you,' I lie.

He grabs my face to inspect the fine art. 'They did it again, huh?'

'I saw you hiding behind the bins. Why didn't you help me?'

'I was gonna wade in, but I needed to take a dump,' he tells me.

I'm clearly not impressed because the bullshit keeps coming. He continues, 'Plus, with my boxing training, my hands are classed as deadly weapons. If I had killed someone, I'd be in deep shit.' Simon's being true to his nickname. He nods to the sweetshop. 'Let's check out the top shelf and get a load of energy drinks.' I ignore him, spit on my hand and turn back to the window and rub my face.

I notice, displayed in the shop front, index cards advertising *'massages'* and *'man with van'* cramped together. My eyes are drawn to one that reads: *Sick and tired of taking a beating? Come to my shop and we'll have a meeting: The Little Shop of Revenge, 10 Pandora Street.*

Simon barges in front of me and examines the cards. 'Sensual massage?' he grins. 'Ha, you'd have to pay double for your two dicks.'

'Why don't you shut your mouth?' I snap. 'All you do is take the piss and tell lies. Boxing training? The closest you've got to the gym is going past it on the school bus.' Simon's face drops. I've never called him out on his lies before, it's too easy, and part of me knows it's wrong, but it feels good to be a dick for a change. I let rip. 'Everyone at school laughs behind your back, they all say how stupid you are. No one believes anything you say, you dumb liar.'

'They don't,' he mumbles.

Simon pushes me, it's pathetic. I shove him back, hard. He spins, his feet tangle and he eats pavement. The thud of his head on the concrete makes me feel sick and I instantly regret it. What am I doing? This *isn't* me. I rush to help him up.

'Get away from me.' Simon pushes me and gets to his feet. He fingers a graze on his forehead, his eyes glassy with tears. 'You're out of order,' he whimpers, before bolting off down the street.

What have I done? I can't stick up to John Peaceman and his gang of ass-hats, but I can be an absolute shit-bag to my best friend. I hang my head and make my way home, hoping the fantasy car that Simon rolled over earlier becomes a reality and squashes me flat. After a while of shuffling along, inspecting the pavement, I realise, instead of heading home, I've ended up on Pandora Street. A large hand-drawn sign with an arrow pointing down an alley reads: The Little Shop of Revenge. I take a second to think how odd this is as I've never been here before, and wouldn't even know how to get here if you asked me. I know I should probably keep heading home, but curiosity gets the better of me.

The shop is true to its name 'Little'. There's a wooden counter with a red buzzer on top, double doors on the back wall and not much else.

A smartly dressed man rises from behind the counter.

'Well come on in, my dear boy," he grins. He walks over to me, his black leather shoes click-clacking on the wooden floor. He offers me his hand, and I shake it. It feels cold, like a freeze pop.

'I'm Horris Drake, the owner of The Little Shop of Revenge. Pleased to meet you.' He lets go of my hand and delves into his top pocket. He removes a fancy handkerchief with the initials HD embroidered on it and motions for me to take it. 'For the male appendage on your face.'

'Thanks.' I take it and scrub the *Venus de penis* from my cheek.

'Ghastly business,' he tuts.

I pass him back the hanky. 'Excellent. Now, as the sign states, this is the place for revenge, and as my name is Horris Drake, the very same name that is on the lease to this fantastic shop, so I do believe it is up to me to assist you with your needs.'

'Not sure I can afford it.'

'Balderdash, Billy,' he beams. *Did I even tell him my name?* 'We can always do business. What do you have in your pockets?'

I rustle through my trousers, removing a folded sheet of paper to get at what little change I have.

'What is that?' he asks, pointing to the paper.

'Oh, this? It's just a drawing I did. It's stupid.'

Horris plucks it from me.

'Nonsense. If you tell people something is stupid, they will be inclined to believe it so. Let them make up their own minds, but in the meantime, assure them everything is fantastically-mind-meltingly-fantastical.' He unfolds the paper, examines it. It's a drawing of me riding a dragon, a buxom princess holding on to me, pushing her boobs against my back.

'So now, if I were to ask you your opinion on this, you'd say… ?' His eyes lock on mine.

'It's… fantastically-mind-meltingly-fantastical?' Each word that leaves my mouth makes Horris's grin widen.

'Yes, I believe it is,' he says, shooting me a wink. 'So it's a deal, I will give you a vessel of revenge, a harbinger of doom, someone to rock someone's socks, in return for your drawing.' He folds it neatly and places it in his pocket.

'Really?' I ask.

'Well of course, how could I turn down something so fantastically-mind-meltingly-fantastical? Now, to business.'

Horris leans on the counter and slaps its shiny wooden surface. 'They say revenge is a dish best served cold, but I say to hell with that, let's microwave it and stuff it down their throats till their bellies burst.'

'Er, sure.'

'I shall now diagnose your case. Stand up straight, look at me, and think unhappy thoughts.' I do as he says. My unhappy thought is John Peaceman.

Horris looks me over. 'Hmmm. Bully. Garden variety. Older than you. Not much of an artist… John is the scoundrel's name,' he says punctuating his announcement with a click-clack of his heels. I don't even have to answer.

'Thought so. I know what you need; or more to the point, what ol' Johnny boy needs.' Horris presses the red button on the counter. Behind him, the double doors part to reveal a hulk of a man, all muscle and tattoos. He jumps up and down like he's gearing up for a fight.

'I give you, cage fighter Crusher Reed. Adept at ferocious fisticuffs, capable of dismantling anyone who is pissing on your chips,' says Horris with game-show host enthusiasm. Crusher unleashes a flurry of super-fast punches into the air, then looks at me.

Crusher speaks. 'I wanna introduce John to my two friends.' He holds up his fists and looks to the left one, 'Punchy,' he says, then looks to the right, 'and Facey.'

'Cool,' I grin.

'Hmm, cool? Cool will not do,' Horris says. He slaps the button and the doors slam shut. He continues, 'No, cool will NOT do at all. It's nowhere near fantastically-mind-meltingly- fantastical. We'll try again.' He hits the red button, the doors slide back. Crusher has been replaced by a huge metal robot with wrecking balls for fists.

'May I present Metal Mike. Two ton of steel revenge. He'll

smash and bash anyone giving you sass and send them to the scrap heap.' Metal Mike smashes the wrecking balls together, the room shakes. His metal jaw clangs open.

'Me crush puny Peaceman.'

Metal Mike is awesome. I'm lost for words. Horris hits the button and the door closes. I protest, 'But–'

'The look on your face said it all. Good, but not great. We will find you something fantastically-mind meltingly-fantastical.' Horris takes the pose of a man deep in thought and I can almost see the light bulb *ping* over his head. 'Got it!' he beams.

'You're a boy who yearns for a personal kind of revenge. *You* want to dish the damage!' Horris hits the button. The doors slide back to reveal… not a cage fighter, not two tons of revenge, but… me.

'May I present the doppelgänger. Looks like you. Sounds like you.'

'Cool,' the other me interrupts, sounding, well, like me.

Horris continues. 'He is one mean little scamp. He'll bite, blight and fight your enemy until they're just a smear on the concrete.'

I think of John being used to paint the pavement, and I feel a Horris-type grin forming.

'Well?' Horris asks.

I say the words, 'He's fantastically…' I imagine John begging for mercy as 'I' smash his face, 'mind-meltingly…' John spewing blood, choking on his own teeth, begging for mercy! 'Fant–' I pause, the sick feeling I felt earlier when Simon banged his head because of my actions floods my stomach. How would I really feel if John was reduced to a puddle of blood and I was responsible?

'Well, boy?' Horris asks.

I step back. 'I'm not sure I want this.'

Horris's grin falters. 'What?'

'Well, John is a dick, but this is… wrong. I can wash the dick off my face, but he'll always be one for the rest of his life, and if I go through with this, I'll be as bad as he is. Worse even.' I'm amazed at how grown-up I sound. My mind turns to Simon. I've been a right twat. I need to apologise and make it up to him.

'I gotta go,' I blurt as I dart for the door.

'Time waster!' Horris hollers.

I exit the alley and sprint back to the sweetshop where I buy energy drinks and sweets for me and Simon as we've both had a day that sucks. I head down Simon's street and see him coming my way.

'I'm sorry,' I shout, and I hold up the bag of goodies. 'I got us a whole ton of the good stuff.'

Simon breaks into a sprint.

I delve into the bag. 'I got you your favouri–'

Simon powers into me, knocking me down. The cans of drink skid into the street. Simon stands over me and rains down punches. One breaks my nose; another shatters teeth. He takes me by the wrist and snaps it left to right loosening my arm from the socket before ripping it off and tossing it over his shoulder. I look up to see someone scoop up one of the cans – it's another Simon, *my Simon.*

He gulps from the can and looks down at me. 'I'm not a dumb liar, Billy. I'm fantastically-mind-meltingly-fantastical.'

PIG

It was a hot day on the farm. Samson the pig was in his pen, his big pig-head resting on the bars of the enclosure looking out over the courtyard. Samson favoured this spot. He could see the whole farm, the farmer's house, the horse stables, the fields filled with sheep, but it was the tin shed next to the farmer's house that held his attention the most. Samson had been studying it for weeks now, trying to figure out what went on inside. He used to think it was a bigger pen for pigs that got too fat, but lately, he had a much more sinister hunch.

The door to the shed clattered open. The farmer stood in the doorway shouting at someone inside. 'Get out of it, ya dirty bird.'

A large crow swooped out through the open door and flew high into the air. It *cawed* at the farmer as if shouting *piss off*.

'Stay out!' the farmer screamed before disappearing inside and slamming the door.

The crow glided over to the pig-pen and perched on the bars by Samson's head. The bird *chirped* and *clicked* in his ear as if sharing juicy gossip. Samson's eyes filled with sadness at what he was hearing.

'Thank you,' he sighed.

Samson pushed his snout into a bundle of straw and uncovered a small chick that *peeped* and hopped in circles. Using his snout, he tossed the yellow fluff into the air. The crow snatched it up in its beak.

'Payment,' Samson grunted. He shuddered and turned his attention back to the pig pen. It was home to many pigs of all different sizes. The bigger pigs lounged in the corners while the piglets leapt and darted like pink lightning bolts.

Samson stomped to the centre of the pen and let out a thunderous *Oink*! 'Everyone, listen. I have something important to tell you.'

The adult pigs pricked up their ears and told the piglets to sit still and behave or they'd get no slop. Samson had the pen's attention and all the pigs looked on, eager to hear what their leader had to say.

'We have to leave. We're not safe here,' he snorted.

'Why?' asked one pig.

'The shed, it's not a bigger pen like we thought it was. The farmer he's–' Samson paused, there were piglets present but this needed to be said. 'He's fattening us up, so he can slaughter us for food.'

The pen fell silent.

'For food?' asked Bullet, one of the more ignorant pigs.

'Yes, eat us. Like slop.'

The air filled with *gasps* and *Weees*.

'But the farmer loves us, takes care of us. Who told you such nonsense?'

'Twitter, the crow,' Samson grunted.

'The crow? Crows are liars,' squealed Bullet.

'And pigs are stupid!' Samson bellowed, stomping his trotter and glaring at him.

Bullet deflated and shuffled back into the crowd.

'Listen to me. Every mouthful of slop you guzzle is taking you closer to your death.' Samson's gaze moved from one pig to the next as he spoke. 'I've been observing what's been going on for months now…' Samson paused and lowered his head. 'The crow just confirmed what I already knew.'

'What are we going to do?' squealed one pig.

'We're leaving tonight. We'll go and live in the woods,' said Samson.

'How will we get out of the pen?'

'I'll take care of it. Rest now; we leave tonight.'

The pigs dispersed, squealing in hushed tones. Samson went back to his spot and rested his head on the bars. He glared at the tin shed.

Bella, Samson's wife, trotted up beside him and rubbed her head against his.

'Are the piglets okay?' he asked her.

'They're piglets, Sam. They think it's an adventure. What did the crow see in there?'

'It doesn't bear repeating.'

Samson's expression softened. He turned to Bella. 'All the pigs taken to that shed, your uncle, my mother and one day, even our own piglets. How could I have been so naïve, Bella? The pigs look to me to lead them.'

Bella nuzzled Samson's neck. 'Why wouldn't we trust the farmer? He feeds us, keeps us warm. Even lets his own child play with us.'

Samson's nostrils flared and he grit his teeth. He boiled at the thought of the farmer's betrayal. 'How could he act as our friend, only to slit our family's throats? What type of animal does that?'

Samson's gaze snapped back to the shed. 'Leave me please, Bella. I need to be alone.'

Bella nodded. 'I love you,' she whispered, but Samson didn't hear. Thoughts of revenge had taken him to a dark place where words of affection couldn't reach.

*

Samson stayed in that same spot for hours, staring at the shack, his mind turning rotten with hatred and the need for revenge. He knew, that later that night the farmer would do his rounds and check the pen – that is when Samson would strike.

*

The moon was high in the sky when Samson's eyes locked onto the farmer making his way towards the pen. Bolt, the sheepdog, followed behind, sniffing at the floor.

'You still up, Sam?' the farmer called.

Samson would normally reply with a grunt, but instead, he just stared through the farmer.

The farmer reached the pen and patted Samson's head. It made Samson feel sick, and a low growl escaped his mouth. The farmer stepped back, puzzled. It was the first time he'd heard a pig make such a sound.

'You getting ill, Sam?'

Bolt sniffed up alongside the farmer, *in striking range of the pen*. Samson thrust his head through the bars and clamped his jaws around Bolt's front legs. *Arooo!* the dog cried as Samson yanked him inside and dragged him to the centre of the pen.

'Bolt!' the farmer screamed. He fumbled for the keys to the gate. Samson released the mutt's mangled legs from his mouth. He looked up at the farmer: *Come and fucking get him!*

The farmer opened the lock and threw open the gate. He raced inside. Samson charged at him and smashed him to the floor. The raging pig pounded him with a trotter and locked his jaw around the farmer's kneecap. With a *crunch,* bone and cartilage shattered inside Samson's mouth.

Samson released him and looked to Bella. 'Go! Lead the pigs to the woods.'

Bella nodded. 'Everyone through the gate!'

A steady stream of pigs dashed out into the courtyard

and fled. Samson circled the farmer and Bolt as they flailed about, their legs broken and useless.

'Sam! Come on,' Bella called.

'Those slaughtered deserve revenge,' he grunted. 'Go. I'll catch up.'

Bella nodded, knowing that to argue would be a waste of time.

Samson turned his attention to Bolt. The dog was licking its mangled legs, picking them up in its mouth and straightening them out as if by doing so he would fix them. He looked up at Samson, confused.

Samson *oinked: I'm sorry*. He placed his gaping mouth around the dog's head and clamped down. Bolt *yelped* as his skull *cracked* and *crunched* between Samson's jaws like it was made of eggshell.

From the corner of his eye, Samson could see the farmer was trying to drag himself away. He spat out the mutt's crushed head and looked beyond the farmer to his house. That is where he would have his revenge.

*

Inside the house, Samson stalked up the stairs. He moved toward the nearest door and bullied his way inside using his snout. In the room lay the farmer's wife, asleep in bed. Thin white sheets covered her legs, leaving the rest of her barrel-like belly exposed to the sticky night air. Memories of Samson's mother came flooding back to him as his pig eyes traced over the farmer's wife's bloated stomach and lingered on two large, saggy teats that flopped down on either side of her doughy frame. Samson *grunted* – he could very much use a drink. He would help himself, just like the farmer helped himself to Samson's loved ones.

Samson lumbered forward and greedily took a teat in his mouth. He sucked hard and fast, but the skin of the farmer's wife was not tough and robust like his mother's and the teat snapped and made an odd popping sound as it burst, sending a gush of hot liquid down his throat. The farmer's wife screamed and jolted back across the bed, her hands cupped against the saggy flap of leaking skin that was once her tit. She lunged for the door, leaving a trail of red and yellow splatter as she tried to escape. Samson slammed her into the wall and went for her ankles. With one powerful chomp, he popped her feet clean off.

The wailing woman dropped to her knees and crashed down. She dragged herself towards the landing, her footless legs glugging blood all over the floorboards.

Samson followed, his large tongue lapping at the blood trail, his eyes locked on her rump that wobbled as she crawled. He sniffed his way up behind her, sank his jaws into the flesh of her arse, ripped off a hunk and swallowed, a thick yellow fat coated his taste buds, causing them to spasm in delight – *people tasted amazing.* He would have another bite. He sank his jaw into the back of her leg, tasty red juice pooled in his mouth and he greedily sucked it down, only for it to replenish again and again.

Samson slurped and chomped, sampling each part of her.

When he'd stripped the flesh from her back and legs, he flipped her over and took the other teat in his mouth, it exploded, covering the roof of his mouth in a thick tasty goo. Samson ears pricked up. He looked away from his banquet.

He'd been in such a feeding frenzy, he hadn't noticed Penny, the farmer's daughter, watching him from her bedroom doorway.

Penny stood, frozen, holding a piglet cuddly-toy to her chest, her eyes glistening with tears.

Samson felt hollow, sickened. Ashamed that one so young had to witness such horror. He backed away from the pile of delicious slop that was now Penny's mother and let out a low *Oink.* If Penny could understand Pig she would have known that Samson was saying: *Sorry. I'm so very sorry.*

He trotted towards her.

*

Samson marched into the courtyard, his skin slick with blood, his belly bulging with meat. He approached the farmer, still trying to drag himself towards the house.

Samson spat a blood-stained piglet toy by the farmer's head.

A look of recognition snapped across the farmer's face. 'No!' he screamed.

Samson gently placed his snout next to the farmer's ear, but instead of speaking Pig, Samson squealed human words.

'How doesss it feeeeeeel?'

MEAT BEN

Ben woke up naked, alone and face down on a rancid scrap of carpet in the back of a freezing van. He tried to push himself up, but his arms felt like they were made of lead and were on loan from someone else.

The van rocked along tackling bumps and potholes. These weren't the manmade streets of London, he thought, they must be out in the country somewhere, far far away from the city. He remembered the night before – getting home from work, showering, eating spaghetti bolognese his mum had sent over for him. All the mundane, trivial things that now in this moment seemed so precious.

Ben remembered someone in his room.

The suffocating smell of chemicals.

He didn't know who had done this to him and he didn't know why, but he did know at some point they'd get to where they were heading, then he'd really be in trouble. He fought to lift his head from the carpet – thick strings of drool poured from his mouth, like tethers trying to hold him in place. He called out but nothing passed his lips.

The van jolted to a halt. Ben's head slammed down nose first with a *crunch.* A flash flood of blood soaked the back of his throat and he coughed and spluttered red gak onto the carpet.

Outside, the squelch of mud grew louder – the back doors of the van cranked open and the smell of cow shit rode in on the morning air. A young, ginger-haired woman in farmhand gear peered in at him. 'Well, hey there, handsome,' she said with a grin. Tucked under the woman's arm was a long pole with a wire loop on the end. A *tut* escaped her as she set eyes on Ben's bloody nose. 'Aw, no. You done yourself a mischief?'

Upfront, the driver's door slammed shut and an obese man with a slab of pale gut hanging from an ill-fitting jacket trudged up beside the woman. 'Hey, Arleen,' he said blowing into his hands and rubbing them together. 'Fresh out here this morning.'

'Hey, big fella. All good?'

'Good as gravy. This un was easy peasy.'

'That's 'cause you got all the moves,' Arleen said giving his arm a nudge.

They stood observing Ben twitching like a freshly swatted fly. 'What a sorry looking thing,' Arleen sighed. 'C'mon, boy. Old Arleen ain't gonna hurt yah.' She extended the pole inside and positioned the loop around Ben's neck. The wire tightened and he was yanked from the van onto the frost-dusted mud. The obese man fumbled in his pockets and pulled out cable ties with a pair of boxer shorts tangled amongst them. The underwear sprang free and fell at his feet.

Arleen shot them a disapproving look. 'And what you been doing with them?' she asked. The man snatched up the underwear and stuffed them back in his pocket.

'He ain't gonna be needing them,' he said, his cheeks bright red.

'And you do, do yah?' Arleen jabbed a finger into his belly. 'I don't think they'd fit. 'less you planning on going on a diet or somethin'?'

The man rubbed his face, trying to wipe away embarrassment. He held up the cable ties to distract. 'I'll tie him good for yah. You watch.' He leant over Ben and tightly zipped his wrists. 'I also fixed his yapper for you.'

Arleen softened. 'Well ain't, you a sweetheart.'

'Want me tah help you get him in?'

'Naw, I'm guessin' you'll be wantin' breakfast after that long drive. But you make sure you keep those under-crackers you done taken to yourself, yah hear? I don't want folk thinkin' we about any funny business here.'

'Yeah, of course, Arleen. 'I promise.'

'Good. You go get. There's meat and fresh bread in the hut for yah.'

'Oh, boy. Thanks.' The man grinned and stomped off into the darkness.

Arleen turned her attention to Ben. She knelt beside him, wiped the blood from his nose with the back of her hand. 'You gonna even try and get up for me, sweetie?'

Ben looked ahead to the fields surrounding them. In his head he was sprinting through the grass, the morning dew soaking his bare feet as he galloped to safety – in reality, he dribbled blood and released a wet fart.

Arleen put a hand on her knee and pushed herself up. 'Jeez, the big fella dosed you good, huh? No matter. Arleen jus' drag yah. Stronger than ah look.' She shouldered the pole and pulled Ben towards the light of an old barn. They passed a pen full of pigs who stared at him with pitch-black eyes. They shoved their snouts through the bars and *oinked* excitedly. Arleen glanced over her shoulder. 'Look at you makin' friends already.' The animals raced along the pen, piling on top of each other, following as far as their enclosure allowed before Arleen and Ben disappeared out of sight and into the barn.

Mud changed to concrete, and the smell of cow shit turned to nostril-burning disinfectant. Ben's bladder gave out and a warm stream of piss spurted over his legs leaving a trail behind them as Arleen pulled him through a dimly lit corridor lined with barn doors. 'Just up ahead, darling,' said Arleen.

She dragged Ben into a room with retina-scorching lights overhead and a grubby tiled floor. Arleen deposited Ben in a scummy shower cubicle. She stood over him, propping him up so his back was against the wall and his legs and feet sat snuggly inside the shower tray. She removed the noose from his neck, lifted it over his head and twisted a tap on the wall. Water surged through the old pipes and the shower head spluttered to life.

'You stay put, now. I'll be right back.' Arleen walked away.

Ben's brain was on fire, cooking the inside of his skull, screaming at his limbs to spring into action. Suddenly, his left leg kicked out, the heel of his foot landing outside the cubicle and thudding on the tiles.

Arleen returned with a broom and a grin. 'Now whatchoo doin' there getting all worked up?' She slid her boot under Ben's calf and flicked his leg back inside the shower enclosure. She thrust the broom at him and raked. 'Gotta wash behind those ears so we don't get no potatoes growing.' Arleen scrubbed, the bristles of the broom leaving tiny cuts on Ben's skin that swelled under the water. She worked the broom back and forth leaving no crevice un-violated until Ben was bright pink. Arleen set the broom down and turned off the shower. Placing her hands on her hips, she admired her handiwork. 'Lookin' real sweet. Think that should do it.' Arleen's gaze fell to Ben's privates. A smile hitched her cheeks. She knelt and rooted between his legs, 'Woo, woo' she said, yanking his shrivelled cock. 'Not much of a tallywhacker on yah. Maybe we should call you Button?'

Ben's legs jolted and fell wide apart like they were trying

to run in different directions. Arleen stood and took a step back. 'You don't like ol' Arleen doing that? I'm just playin' with you.'

Ben locked eyes with her and let out a low whine that rode a thick wad of spit over his lips. It ran down his chin and splatted onto the tip of his cock that had started to react to the warmth of Arleen's touch. Arleen regarded the unfurling strip of flesh with disgust. 'Now I don't stand for none of that, mister.' She grabbed the broom and gave Ben's unwanted semi a whack, squishing it against the bottom of the shower tray – pain ate at Ben's groin, he gasped for air like a fish snatched from its tank.

'You tryin' a speak?' Arleen asked.

She picked up a mirror from a metal shelf and knelt between Ben's legs. Arleen pushed her face close to his. 'Shh, shh, there, Button,' she said pressing her thumb against Ben's creased brow. 'Let's work those bad feelings outta there.' Her fingers smoothed down his cheek and locked around his jaw – Arleen yanked Ben's mouth open and showed him his reflection – a swollen stump of flesh where his tongue used to be. His guts churned. Arleen worked Ben's jaw, *'I'm sorry, Arleen, for being bad,'* she said in a cartoonish high-pitched voice. *'It's just, you the purdiest gal I ever seen.'* Arleen slammed Ben's mouth shut and slapped him gently under the chin. 'You stop being silly, Button. You can't talk with no yapper.'

Ben's screaming brain finally connected with his limbs – his arms jerked towards the mirror, smashing it into Arleen's face. She stumbled back, her feet finding the broom, sending her head first onto the tiles and out cold.

Ben launched himself from the cubicle. His body slammed down spraying water and blood – the room had been hidden when he was in the shower but now, under the harsh lights, he could see it for what it was. He was in some kind of operating theatre. Scalpels and medical gear glittered on a tray next to an operating table stained with blood, the red on sheets looking like some twisted Rorschach test. On the wall, behind an assortment of breathing apparatus, was a diagram of the human body, the muscles and veins shown in great detail.

Ben flexed his hands against the cable-tie around his wrists but the sharp edges dug into his skin. Ben squirmed around and pointed himself towards the exit. He wriggled and thrashed towards the doorway like a salmon fighting the current. He reached the opening and clamped his hands around the frame using it to pull himself up. Leaning out into the corridor, he could see the dim light from naked bulbs hinting at pathways branching either side. Ben's panic grew as he realised he had no idea how to get out. He then saw the faint trail of piss still staining the concrete. He hurled himself away from the frame and staggered along the corridor following the piss line.

Arleen sat up and held her throbbing head. 'Gosh darn it.' She got to her feet, sending tiny pieces of glass falling from the creases in her jacket. She brushed herself off and wiped blood from her eye. 'What a hoo-haw.' She kicked the broom away from her and marched over to a rusty locker.

Ben's lungs were lava.

He jerked along, fighting to get his legs working as a team instead of against each another – each leg doing its own thing, throwing the other off its stride and wasting time. He turned a corner and slammed into the wall, sliding along it for several jerks.

'I'm comin' for yah,' Arleen called, her cheery voice echoing not far behind.

Out of gas, Ben slid down onto his knees – the trail of piss stretched far along the corridor, the exit still out of sight. On the opposing wall, a line of wooden doors numbered with bright red paint offered a place to hide. He willed himself up and lunged towards the closest one.

Ben fell through into darkness.

His eyes struggled to adjust and make sense of the grey shapes in the black surrounding him. He was in some sort of animal enclosure judging by the overpowering stench of shit. At the far end of the room, a shard of blue morning light crept in through a broken window. He stumbled towards it, passing cages shrouded in darkness, his movements setting off *Grunts* and *Sniffs* from the inhabitants. Behind him, the door banged open, light from the hallway barged inside. 'Whare yo goin', mister?' called Arleen. 'Now I know you upset, but that's no reason to mash mah face, now is it? Jus' darn rude.'

Something sharp struck Ben's rump. His body locked, his legs turned to ballast and the floor raced to meet him, filling his mouth with dirt and his head with pain.

'Tut, tut, tut, you big silly. You can't git away from me. I git you with mah darts,' said Arleen, her words punctuated with the ping and fizz of lights firing up. Section by section the dark gave up its secrets. The grunts weren't coming from animals. They were coming from *people*. Ben was in a barn surrounded by cages, each one home to someone or some*thing* mutilated and hacked. The few who still had legs raced around their cells releasing high pitch *gurgles,* throwing themselves into the bars. Some cages were silent but for the sound of breathing apparatus keeping their dying bodies clinging to life – their eyes still twitching, observing the horror inflicted on them. 'Everyone jus' calm down now,' said Arleen as she approached.

Ben couldn't tear his gaze away from the cage closest to him.

A wooden sign tied to the bars, a crudely painted flower with the word *Buttercup* on it. Inside slept what was left of a young woman. Buttercup was just a head and torso with four smooth stumps jutting from where her limbs once were. Ben's stomach burned, acid and spew gushed from his mouth. Buttercup's eyes snapped open. She locked eyes with him through a nest of matted blonde hair. She grinned and began working her way along, wriggling, towards the edge of her cage.

Arleen's shadow cast over Ben. 'You aint getting in mah good books with all this hoo-haw.'

Buttercup poked her head out between the bars letting out an exited *wheezing* sound. Arleen met her with a grin 'Hey, darlin.' She said. She knelt down and softly scratched Buttercup around her neck. A content smile stretched its way across the mutilated woman's face. Arleen turned to Ben 'You should be ashamed of yourself, disturbin' this young missy.' Arleen reached into the cage and patted her bloated belly. 'She due in a few weeks.'

*

Ben woke in a cage of his own on a bed of straw, his eyelids heavy, and his mouth so dry it felt like it would crack if moisture touched it. He reached into his mouth to confirm what he already knew and touched the dry mound of swollen flesh where his tongue used to be. His fingers fumbled along his gums – his teeth now absent too. Ben pressed his mouth of swollen flesh together and looked through a wall of tears to the cage opposite. Buttercup lay in the corner, fast asleep on a bed of soiled hay. He looked her over, at her sagging teats, her bloated stomach, the flies buzzing around her vagina.

Somewhere a door opened and footsteps echoed around the enclosure. Ben retreated to the corner of his cage and pulled armfuls of straw over himself. He could hear Arleen approaching. 'You got yourself a girlfriend yet?' she said.

'No. Girls don't really like me,' replied a young man.

'They be silly girls then. Good lookin' boy like you. They should be snapping you up.'

'Thanks, Arleen. You're always so kind to me.'

Arleen and a goofy looking young man in a backwards baseball cap paused in front of Ben's cage. 'This is the new-un. I call him Button. I figure we can get most of whatcha be needin' offa him. Needs a bit of calmin' down.'

The young man nodded and consulted the clipboard by his side. 'I need a couple of foot of skin. A kidney and six pints of the red stuff,' he said.

Arleen nodded, considered the request. 'What type?'

'Huh?'

'The red stuff, what type?'

'Oh.' The young man scanned the clipboard, '... Erm, B Negative.'

'Horndog down in cage two will do you for that.' She glanced at Ben. 'This un here's A plus. Sweetpea, cage ten will do for the skin, she big as a barn and we'll have better chance o' getting it off in one piece,' Arleen said as the young man took notes. She stepped towards Ben's cage and peered through the bars. Ben stared back through a shaking blanket of straw. She locked eyes with him and smiled. 'We'll have to use Verne down in cage three for the kidney, 'bout the only thing he got left to give.' Arleen pushed her hand through the bars and wagged a finger at Ben. 'You off the hook today, but I'm thinkin' they'll be something on next week's order you can help with to make up for all that drama you caused.'

'Oh, and there's a request for a videotape recording...'

Arleen pulled her hand from the cage and turned to the young man. She looked at him inquisitively waiting for more information. The boy's pimple-ravaged skin flushed red and he looked to the floor.

'Well? Spit it out. Video of what?' Arleen asked.

The young man held the clipboard up for Arleen to see. 'I rather not say it out loud.'

Arleen studied the board. The more she read the higher her eyebrows rose and stretched the ginger freckles on her nose. 'I swear orders jus' keep getting stranger and stranger.' She handed the board back.

'Can we even do that? It possible?'

'Well o' course. They paying ain't they?' Arleen turned and glared at Ben in his cage. 'You gonna be a movie star, Button. I got just the part for you... and you got just the parts for me.'

THE BAD SLICE

Margarita Monday!

Twenty percent off all Margarita Pizzas!

I drag my feet across the carpark not just because I like the sound of gravel beneath my trainers, but because part of me wants to trip and knock myself unconscious so I don't have to work today. Unfortunately, I make it to the back door and enter the Pizza Palace staffroom. Franco, my boss, calls it the staffroom but that's an oversell, it's just a room with a damp problem, a table, a few chairs and a beaten-up locker he found abandoned in the car park.

Melvin is at the table, mesmerised, his nose inches away from a mobile phone, the speakers straining with the sound of squawking and groaning.

'What's that?' I ask.

'Your mum.' Melvin grins. I peek over his shoulder; he's watching porn again. A guy dressed as a pterodactyl is going caveman on a cavewoman.

'That's weird even for you,' I say.

A locker slams behind me, Kenzy pushes his hair back and pulls a Pizza Palace cap over his head. 'You think that's weird? Look at that bloody thing,' he says nodding to the corner. Between the bundles of flatpack Pizza Palace pizza boxes and a racking system that looks like it's about to collapse, is a five-foot-tall triangular slice of pizza with eyes the size of frisbees and a toothpaste *'ting'* grin. Imagine if a guy fucked a pepperoni pizza and that pizza gave birth to a mutant-sized slice with a fuck-you smile and a pair of cartoon eyes then you're pretty much there.

'What did I miss?' I ask.

'Mr Pappa-roni,' says Melvin as pterodactyl man reaches climax – dinosaurs roar, a volcano erupts. I'm still none the wiser. 'It's the restaurant's new mascot,' he continues. 'Disneyland has Mickey Mouse. Pizza Palace gets Mr Pappa-roni.'

'Franco's idea,' says Kenzy. 'He came up with the name.'

'It's stupid,' says Melvin tucking his phone into his pocket.

The door to the kitchen opens, the smell of freshly-cooked frozen pizza wafts in. Franco's in the doorway, his gut testing the buttons on his shirt. 'Greg, you're fucking late.'

I jab a finger into the rubbery surface of the giant slice. 'What's up with this?'

'Promotion for the store. Mr Pappa-roni here is going to bring in more customers.'

I look at the random red circles on the rubber surface; they are more like blisters than slices of succulent pork and beef sausage. 'This looks pretty worn,' I say fingering holes in the side that have red stains around them.

'It was used at another pizza store,' Franco says.

'Where, in a soldier's PTSD nightmare?' I look closer at the marks. 'This looks like blood.'

'Shut your shit. It's tasty tomato sauce. Now get ready for work. It's Mr Pappa-roni's first day.'

Melvin takes his phone from his pocket again and slumps even further in his chair until his chin is almost level with the table top. 'It's really stupid.'

Franco moves in. 'No, Melvin your dad's stupid, he

bedded a stupid girl, and they had a stupid baby, that stupid baby grew up to work for me, and that's why you're gonna wear it first.'

'I'm pretty sure you can't talk to us like that, Franco,' says Kenzy.

'Feel free to make a complaint to HR.' Franco grabs his crotch. 'They just relocated to my balls. You've got to shout loud into my dick so they can hear you.' Franco pushes the door open using a combination of elbow and foot like he's in fucking Happy Days or something and twirls away.

The door slams leaving the three of us staring at Mr Pappa-roni.

'Why do I get all the shit jobs?' asks Melvin.

'We work in Pizza Palace, Melv. Every job's a shit job,' I say.

'Twenty minutes,' Kenzy says, checking his look in the spot of the mirror that has the least grime on it. He arranges his hair perfectly around the edges of his cap. He looks like he should be a model or something, not here, stuck out back working the ovens.

'Twenty minutes what?' asks Melvin.

'In the costume. You're going to get hot in there. You shouldn't spend more than twenty minutes inside it. My ex used to get paid to wear a Japanese cat costume at festivals. She would do twenty minutes then take a break, or she'd start to feel nauseated like she was going to faint.'

'What the fuck does nauseated mean?' asks Melvin.

'Feeling sick.'

'Ah, spuking. One more question,' Melvin says. 'Did you ever rump her while she was still in the suit?'

*

Half an hour later, me and Tony are on the tills. He arrived ten minutes after me, but Tony gets a pass as Franco's dating his mum. I try to make conversation, but it's always hard. He's not autistic, but he's definitely on the spectrum. I watch him as he pushes his finger into the screen, making it warp different colours.

'What are you doing?' I ask.

'There's a rainbow in the computer, Greg, a rainbow.'

'You probably shouldn't do tha–'

'Look, cheese Melvin is back!' he shouts pointing outside.

Melvin's been inside Mr Pappa-roni handing out leaflets for twenty-five minutes now. At first, he was prancing around doing stupid dances, full of energy but I guess he's getting tired because when we see him again, he's just shuffling around aimlessly like a soldier on the beaches of Normandy that's just had the back of his head blown off. We watch him through the window, his yellow lycra-covered arms by his side, no more leaflets in his white foam-bloated gloves. Even his legs are wrapped in lycra. I can only imagine how much sweat is pooling in those big red boots.

Mr Pappa-roni shuffles to a stop, his big cartoon eyes slowly tracking people left and right as they go by. I watch him for a moment and call out. 'Melvin, come take a break!' but he ignores me or just can't hear.

'Can I have a medium margarita and some garlic bread, please,' a customer asks, drawing my attention. I tap the order on my screen. 'It's twenty per cent off today, right?'

'Absolutely, it's margarita Monday here at Pizza Palace,' I reply in my cheesiest promotional voice. 'That's eight-fifty, please.' The woman hands me the money, and I crack open the till. 'That'll only be a moment,' I tell her handing her back the change.

She steps away and eyeballs her phone while she waits.

I look back out to Mr Pappa-roni. He still hasn't moved from his spot and is still scanning passers-by. Only now I notice that one of Mr Pappa-roni's arms is empty, just a thin strip of yellow lycra weighted down by an oversized white glove. I also see that it's not all the people he's tracking... just the women – the attractive ones. He starts shaking like an electrical current is shooting through him, his knees bending and knocking together.

'Greg, does cheese Melvin need a wee?' Tony asks.

A loud beep behind me signals the order's ready. I force myself to look away and grab it from the hot plate. A bang from the front of the store makes me turn my head back so fast my jaw takes a second to catch up – Mr Pappa-roni has collided with a table and calamities through the restaurant. He completes three full spins before face-planting the floor.

The woman screams, or maybe it's Tony. I dart around the counter and knee-slide over the tiles to Melvin's side, pushing him onto his back, and I sink my fingers into the Velcro on the side of the costume. With a *riiipp* I yank it open, the heat hits me like the time I opened the dishwasher and poked my head in too soon, and then the smell hits me as if I'd filled that dishwasher with tramps' arseholes.

Ignoring the smell, I wrestle him from the costume, its weight keeping it in place as I help give birth to a pale, sweat-marinated Melvin. He resembles a newborn calf, all weak and covered in gunk – I drop him and scuttle back across the floor – in his hand, also gasping for air, in a vice-tight grip, is his pasty white cock, his knuckles and Pizza Palace shirt glazed with cum.

Melvin has wanked himself unconscious.

Spicy-Wedge Tuesday!

Free wedges with every order over ten pounds!

Tuesday morning, it's so hot the sun has turned my car into a bug oven. A few dead flies rock back and forth on the dash as I park in my usual spot behind Pizza Palace. I leave my window cracked an inch to let some air in. After some dedicated foot-dragging and gravel displacing, I'm back in the staffroom, feeling like I only left an hour ago. I'm greeted by Tony gurning in the mirror while holding a gun under the sink. I freeze and wonder if Tony's finally gone postal and is going to put us all out of our misery, but cancel a retreat when I realise it's only a water pistol that he's filling. 'What's that for?' I ask.

'When I get hot at the till. I'm gonna spray myself.'

I think about cracking a joke, something about better spraying yourself with that than what Melvin sprayed himself with, but I don't. Instead, I say, 'Yeah, good idea,' without a hint of sarcasm. Kenzy's at the table going through clothes and cleaning gear that he's raided from the stockroom. 'Morning,' I say. He looks up, concerned.

'Who farted in your soup?' I ask.

'I wish they had,' Kenzy says. 'I've got to wear the suit today.' He points to the twisted thing at the back of the room, the look on its pizza-face like it's listening and relishing the idea. 'I've scrubbed the hell out of it, but it still stinks inside.'

'If it's any consolation most of Melvin's spunk was absorbed by his Pizza Palace work clothes,' I say. Tony does a snot-bubble laugh so big I hear it pop.

'It's not fucking funny, Tony,' Kenzy snaps. 'I'm sorry,' he says almost instantly out of guilt. We always agreed we could be mean to each other, but never Tony. It wouldn't be right.

Tony doesn't turn from the sink but nods his head and mutters something to himself. Kenzy gets up and pulls me aside. 'Melvin called me last night,' he whispers. 'He told me he thinks the suit did something to him.'

'To him? He turned that costume into a wank furnace. Franco should rehire him and get him to cook the pizzas,' I suggest, but Kenzy's not amused.

'He says he didn't have any control over what he was doing.'

'Oh, come on. I'd hear him whacking off all the time in the men's. The kid has a problem.' It's true, he does.

Franco enters the room followed by the cheesy smell of the shop floor. He slaps Tony's shoulder. 'Tony, my man, you're on the counter.' He looks at the gun in Tony's hands. 'That's not real right?' I can't tell if he's asking a genuine question or joking around. Tony fires two squirts into the sink, and Franco is satisfied. 'Ah, good. Keep that back here, buddy.'

'Why can't Tony wear the suit?' asks Kenzy.

'He's claustrophobic. His mum says he... he just can't wear the thing okay? Greg, you're on the counter. Kenzy you're in the suit.' Franco does a Happy Days back out to the shop floor.

Kenzy turns to me. 'I'm only doing twenty minutes at a time. I don't want to get too hot and fry.'

Tony's waves the water pistol in Kenzy's face. 'If you get too hot I'll come out and squirt you.'

'Thank's, Tony. That's great,' Kenzy says humouring him. 'Greg, don't let me be in it for more than twenty minutes. Keep an eye on your watch.'

*

At the counter, things are slow. Too hot for sizzling pizza. I watch Kenzy outside, handing out flyers, baking in the bastard heat. He has been inside Mr Pappa-roni for almost twenty minutes, and he hasn't taken to wanking in him which is good as my knees still have burns from my floor slide. Franco had to give the woman free pizza for a year to keep quiet about what she saw, although I'd question the judgement of a woman who would accept food from a place with a masturbating pizza-slice for a mascot.

At his till Tony tears napkins into little people and draws faces on them. He looks so happy in his little world. 'Want to make some?' he asks, noticing my interest. He pushes a wad of napkins towards me.

'Maybe, when I get back. I've got to use the bogs. You okay for a minute?' Tony nods, deep in concentration, drawing what looks like a fedora on a napkin Indiana Jones. 'Thanks, Tony.' I step around the counter and notice Mr Pappa-roni has vanished. 'When Kenzy comes back into view, call him in, will you?'

*

I'm in the men's trying not to urinate on the frozen cake thing as it's a deflector shield for piss, and I don't want to get splashback on my dark green Pizza Palace company-issue trousers. I tuck my wang away and step back into a wall that wasn't there before – spinning around I almost fall back into the urinal – Mr Pappa-roni is here with me. 'Jesus Christ Kenzy, what the fuck are you doing?' I check my watch. 'You've been in there for over twenty now. Take a break.' He doesn't move or reply. 'I'm not peeling you out of that shit if you take a dive.'

'I like it in here,' he tells me, his voice low and distant like he's lost in a cave somewhere. I look into the slit below the fake eyes and look at his real ones, beads of sweat race down his forehead.

'You're sweating balls,' I say.

'I really like it in here.'

'Wow, that's awesome. Can I wash my fucking hands now?' I try to move around him, but he blocks me.

'Let's hurt Tony.'

'What?'

'Let's hurt him real bad and stuff him in the oven,' Kenzy says in a very un-Kenzy way.

'Stop being fucking stupid and get out of my way.'

'We don't have to turn it on, I mean we could but… we won't. But we could.'

'Kenzy, you're not known for being funny, you're the sensible one in this dump. Stay in character.'

Kenzy pulls a knife from behind his back. 'Maybe we could just cut him up then?' The toilet door squeals open, Kenzy turns, I panic and take my chance knocking the knife from his foam fingers, sending it spinning under the shit cubicles.

Tony pokes his head in. 'Greg, can you come hel–'

Kenzy leaps, but I grab him by the crust and pull him to the floor before he gets close. I trip and land on top of him, knocking a belly full of wind out of him that escapes through the eye slot.

'Get the fuck off me, you idiot,' Kenzy screams.

Tony's head vanishes behind the door.

'Calm down!' I shout. Mr Pappa-roni's hands clamp around my neck and squeeze. My fingers find the Velcro on the side of the suit and worm their way in. I tear it open, feeling the heat escape over my knuckles. I knock Kenzy's arms away and prise the costume open like a coffin lid. 'Calm the fuck down, dude!' I shout again, exposing him.

We lock eyes, Kenzy gasps for air and stops fighting.

'What? I didn't mean… what was I doing?'

He looks like he's been hollowed out and stuffed with ghosts.

I take a breath, kick myself away across the floor and rest against the urinal.

Franco marches in with Tony in tow.

*

We are all bundled into Franco's office, Kenzy next to me, his head in his hands, Mr Pappa-roni in the corner, on the floor because he's not real and doesn't need a fucking chair. Franco looks at us from behind his desk. 'What the fuck you two? You scared Tony.'

'I didn't mean to. I don't know what happened,' mutters Kenzy.

'Jesus Christ you sound like Melvin. No one knows shit do they?' Franco says.

'I think Kenzy just panicked, got too hot,' I add. 'I was helping him get out of it.' I don't mention the oven stuff or the knife. Franco still fires Kenzy. I get off with a warning.

In the staffroom, I help Kenzy clear out his locker.

'I remember being out front and then I had this urge to… I… I can't explain it,' he tells me as he opens up his man-bag a broken man. He slowly empties the study books from his locker into his bag. He did tell me what he was studying for once, but I plain forget.

'You had a knife, dude. Are you fucking nuts?'

Kenzy looks at me, his eyes still red from the crying. 'I'm so sorry,' he says, looking like he's about to gush again. 'I'd never hurt anyone.'

'And you didn't, dude. You just… overheated, got a little excited.'

Kenzy gives me a weak smile. 'Thanks, Greg.'

Moments later, after an awkward hug, Kenzy gets in his car and grinds gravel.

One Free Topping Wednesday!

You get the idea!

Carpark, gravel, staffroom. Same old shit. I enter and throw my gear into a locker. I take Kenzy's as it's bigger than mine and has less bubblegum plastered inside. Tony walks in eying the floor. 'Hey, you okay, big man?' I ask. Tony nods. 'Hey, Kenzy was just confused you know. I don't even think he knew it was you that walked into the toilets. Either way, I know he's sorry,'

'Okay, thank you.' Tony sits and checks his phone.

Franco waltzes in on a cloud of cheezy fumes. 'Got a new employee coming in today. Her name's Amanda. I've had enough of all the wanking and fighting, or whatever the hell it is you were trying to do Tuesday. I'm going to show her the till. So, Greg, you're in the suit.'

I wish I'd tried harder to trip and smash my fucking brains out in the carpark. 'You've got to be fucking kidding,' I say.

'You're still under review. I could still fire you too, you know. It was only because my main man here, Tony, said you stuck up for him when your little horseplay session got out of hand.'

'Can't we just forget about the suit? It's not–'

'Customers love it.' Franco gives a thumbs-up and jams it towards the ceiling. 'Sales have gone up!'

'I'm not getting in it,' I say.

'Well, then you're not getting paid.'

'This is fucking–'

'Do you wanna take it up with HR?' His hand hovers over his balls ready to crack a dick joke. I think about telling him to go fuck himself, but I need the money – hunger and the idea of going to live under the nearest bridge play a big factor in my life choices.

'Okay, but I'm only doing it for short periods. Then I'm taking smoke breaks. Don't want to be breathing in that shit for too long,' I tell him.

'Good,' Franco replies. Pep-talk over he heads back out to the floor.

Tony follows. 'See, you out there Greg.'

'Yip.' I look at the suit and stare into its big stupid eyes. I peel back the Velcro and open it up like the rubber casket it is. If I ever wondered what the inside of a pizza's arsehole would smell like, I now know – it smells like any other arsehole, of arse. I drag the heels of my shoes against the carpet tiles one after the other and kick them over to the lockers. I set my watch's alarm for fifteen minutes and slide my legs inside Mr Pappa-roni, filling out the yellow tights and stamping my feet into the red clumsy-fuck shoes. I feed my arms in, my fingers finding the gloves and bringing the hands to life. I adjust myself so my eyes are level with the slit and feed the Velcro together to seal myself inside. Plodding across the room, I'm surprised at how heavy all this is and how quickly you get used to the smell. I go out through the restaurant past Tony at the till.

'Go get 'em Mr Pappa-roni,' he yells.

For some reason, I salute him. 'I'm Mr Papp-roni! Come on into Pizza Palace and grab a pizza of the action,' I shout in a stupid voice, Tony grins and all of a sudden I feel oh-so-clever.

Maybe this is going to be fun after all.

*

Outside, I arse around for a while with people on the street, handing out flyers and saying my catchphrase. I even pose for a photo with some woman and her kid. I don't feel the need to put anyone in the oven or masturbate or anything like that. I do however have a fantastic idea. It would be great if I get something sharp and driv–

BEEP. BEEP. BEEP

My watch goes nuts. Time's up. It kills my train of thought, and I struggle to remember what I was thinking. I head inside and give Tony another salute. He salutes back, and the new girl on the tills rolls her eyes like we're the lamest people ever.

I enter the staffroom and peel off the Velcro, emerging from the suit gasping for air like a free diver who went too far down. I snap my arms out of the lycra and pull the boots off my feet.

Franco pokes his head around the door, eyeing me like I might explode any second or sprout tits on my chin. 'You okay?'

'Yeah,' I nod, wiping sweat from my brow.

He looks me over. 'Good. Dick's in your pants, and you're not trying to fight anyone, nice job.' With that nugget of cheer dispensed, he's gone. That's the best thing he's ever said to me: 'nice job'. Nice job for not wanking or fighting. The sort of thing you'd say to a child – *nice job for not shitting your pants, Henry*.

Still, it makes me feel good about myself.

Go me.

*

Wednesday nights I always lock up with Tony. Staff members whose mums aren't getting railed by Franco aren't allowed keys, so Tony supervises while I check that all the ovens and fryers are off. I kill the lights, set the alarm and wait outside with Tony while he locks the staffroom door and pockets the key. We both listen for the alarm pips to make sure Pizza Palace is protected from burglars who would break in and help themselves to pizza.

'Goodnight, Mr Pappa-roni,' Tony tells me pulling his oyster card from a wallet attached to a chain on his trousers. 'You're my favourite one because you didn't touch your meat or try to scare me.'

'Thanks. That means a lot to me.' Tony waves goodbye as if I'm across the street and not just two feet away, then wanders off humming a tune which I'm sure is the opening theme to Ninja Turtles, but I could be wrong. I light a cigarette, breathe that nicotine hit and enjoy the breezy night air infused with the scent of rotten food from the bins.

'Hey.'

I jump and almost swallow my cig. Melvin emerges from the bushes.

'Jesus, fuck, Melvin. Stalk much?'

'I knew you'd be here. I saw on FB that Franco shitcanned Kenzy.'

'Yeah, Kenzy... had a moment. ' I compose myself and take a drag.

'I spoke to him. It was that fucking pizza slice that did it,' Melvin says. He's really reaching here. I feel for Melvin I really do. We've all jacked off in odd places – he just got caught. Melvin pulls his phone from his hoody and taps the screen. 'I need to show you something,' He holds it up for me, the little loading circle-thing rotates slowly. 'Fucking network, man. You got a cigarette?' he asks. I hand him the pack. 'Thanks.'

I look back at the screen – it's still loading. 'Marv, I'm glad to see you, but if you drove five miles to show me two T-rexs jerking off–'

'I don't drive. I rode my BMX, and it's six miles.'

Melvin's phone finally gets its shit together. 'Look,' he says pointing to the screen –a video of a woman in a witch's costume, deep wounds on her chest ooze blood. At first, I think it's fake, but the swollen red holes where her eyes should be look all too real – the camera sweeps over a floor littered with bodies, battered and mutilated, everyone dressed up as different characters. A minimum-effort Pikachu with multiple stab wounds is slumped over a fat, jawless Batman while a fox lady's expression is exactly the one you'd make if you were cradling your entrails – this is the sort of shit you can't unsee.

'Melvin, this–'

'Wait, look.' Melvin jabs the screen with a stiff finger. Mr Pappa-roni, or a suit that looks like Mr Pappa-roni sits in the middle of it all. A giant pizza slice in a sea of blood and bodies, the same toothpaste '*ting*' smile, a cleaver in one hand and a Yoda head in the other. In this context, that smile just looks fucking demented. 'That's our suit!' Melvin says. He pinches the screen, zooms in, and on the side of this Mr Pappa-roni are puncture marks, just like the ones stained with 'tasty tomato sauce' on the Pizza Palace suit.

'What is this shit, Melv?'

'Police footage I found on the web. This guy, Jeffery Fettal. He went to a fancy dress party in the Mr Pappa-roni costume and went nuts. Slaughtered everyone, then vanished.'

'I don't know, Melv.'

'It's true. There was so much blood it trickled down the stairs into the street. People were stepping in it. That's when they called the police.' If Melvin's joking he's hiding it well. 'There's more. The costume went into the police evidence lock-up, and a week later the guard checked it out, wore it home, killed his whole fucking family then just disappeared.'

I laugh, more for effect than because it's funny. 'It reeks

of CreepyPasta to me, Melvin. Besides, making you jack-off and giving Kenzy an odd turn isn't exactly murder, is it?'

'Kenzy told me about the knife.'

'He did?'

'What if you hadn't stopped him?'

'Look, I've been inside Mr Pappa-roni three times today. I'm fine,' I say. Melvin's visibly freaked, and pulls the hood from his head and looks past me to Pizza Palace.

'Did it make you do anything weird?' he asks.

'No. What are you doing?'

'Seeing if there's a trail of bodies behind you or if I can smell burning flesh coming from the kitchen,' he says, without a hint of humour. 'How long were you in it?'

'About fifteen minutes each time.'

Melvin uploads this information to his brain. 'Kenzy said he was in it for around twenty-five minutes, I was in it for less. You were in it for even less than that.'

'So?' I flick my butt and grind it into the gravel.

'Maybe it's a time thing? The longer you're inside, the more control it gets.'

'Bullshit, Melvin. It sounds like the plot of a shitty horror film, or some gory trash a fucking moron would write.'

'I think it makes people do things, Greg. I really do.' Melvin pulls out a key. 'Here, it's the key to the staff room. I jacked it ages ago so I could steal pizza and toilet roll. You have it now. You've got to get rid of that thing. Put it in your car and burn it in the woods. Mess the place up. Franco will think Tony fucked up, and some opportunists got in. You'll never have to wear the suit again.'

Melvin pushes the key into my hand.

'I'm getting out of town,' he says.

'Why, you worried Mr Pappa-roni will get you?'

'The only person I'm worried about is you. I've got to leave town… you get caught wanking in the street, people don't forget that in a hurry.'

'I get it,' I say.

'Take care, Greg.' Melvin pulls his bike from the bushes, hops on and kicks the pedals into position.

'Melv?'

'Yeah?'

'You really rode all the way out here because you're worried about me?'

'Yeah, I guess. Don't go getting all teared up or nothing though.'

'You're a good person. I think you're mentally ill, but still…'

Melv gives me the finger and smiles. He races to the edge of the carpark and does a hard turn back towards me, sending dust into the air. 'Get rid of it, Greg. It's a bad slice.'

Then he's gone.

Pizza Insanity Thursday!

Buy one pizza, get one free!

It's my night off and I'm at home doing my best to leave a dent in the sofa and build a citadel of fizzy drinks cans and sweet packets on my haggard coffee-table. I change the channel for the gazillionth time, my mind more on Melvin and what he showed me. I think he's a fucking nut, but I can't argue that things would be better if there was no suit – I could be back on the till come the morning. I consider going to Pizza Palace and burning me a pizza but decide to eat more crisps instead.

I go to the cupboard.

I'm out of crisps.

*

Parking across the road from Pizza Palace, the big green white and red sign beams in the night like a beacon to passing pissheads. I wait. After two cigarettes and fifteen minutes it switches off, the last customers stumble out through the door, and the place shuts down for the night. Inside, under warm light, Amanda wipes down the counter as Tony hovers. I turn the radio on low and light another smoke. Eventually, Tony pootles down the alley from the carpark and waits at the bus stop until the bus screeches up and whisks him away.

Now's my chance.

I creep around the back of Pizza Palace, give the gravel-crunching a rest and let myself into the staffroom using Melvin's stolen key. Leaving the lights off, I head straight for Mr Pappa-roni. His foam crust bulges between my fingers as I drag his heavy pizza-arse, his big rubber donkey boots following on stretched, thin strips of lycra – I get halfway across the room and go from pulling to pushing to see if he's easier to move, but it's almost like he's clinging to the carpet knowing what's in store for him. I think of all the noise he's going to make outside, being dragged over the gravel – easier just to put him on.

Mr Pappa-roni's unmistakable smell fingers my nostrils as I break the seal on his side. He grins up at me through the dark like he's got his own way. 'Last fucking time,' I mutter. I open him up and feed my legs inside through the lycra until they fill the boots.

'The boss Franco's a pervert, he keeps checking out my tits.'

Holy shit, someone's still in the restaurant.

In a panic, I close myself inside Mr Pappa-roni and punch my hands out through the armholes, through the lycra and into the gloves, all the time thinking what an idiot I am for not realising the alarm wasn't even armed when I came in. I scramble, squeezing back into the corner.

Amanda walks into the staffroom and the lights flicker to life. 'And there's a retarded kid called Tony.'

I watch her through my pizza slit.

'Surprised they let you lock up on your own,' says some big dude with a skinhead and wild, unkempt beard. He looks like he just got off a Viking ship after a successful pillage. I don't know who he is, but I know he's not employed here.

'I told him I wanted to prove myself by locking up on my own, and if he let me do that, I might go on a date with him.'

'Oh, really?' Beardy McFuckface says.

'Yeah, I thought I'd treat my baby to some free pizza and have a little fun.'

Beardy corners her by the table, his arms either side of her. They look into each other's eyes. He plants a kiss on her, hard and fast, like a fox snatching a chicken wing from a hole in a rubbish sack. 'Oh, I see. You want dessert first?' Amanda asks, unbuttoning her Pizza Palace standard issue work polo and pulling it over her head. I don't look at her tits, honest. Instead, I look at the clock: *eleven fifteen*.

They fuck for ages. I learn that Amanda sounds like a chipmunk when she's having sex and the dude's name is either 'Yes!' or 'Boyd' because those are the only two things she keeps moaning. I also learnt that no matter how hard you try, sometimes you can't ward off an erection.

After twenty-five minutes, finally, they stop. They pick

their clothes from the floor and get dressed. 'What the fuck is this shit?' says Boyd, finally noticing me. He walks over and stands inches away, adjusting his top. I pray he or Amanda doesn't notice that Mr Pappa-ronni's arms and legs are fully fleshed-out.

'Oh, that's Mr Margarita,' Amanda says. I feel like coming to life and shouting *the name's Mr Pappa-roni, you fucking stupid bitch,* but I don't. 'Some dipshit called Greg wears it. Do you want some pizza bites? I'll go turn the fryer on.'

'Yeah, sure,' Boyd says, adjusting his collar.

Amanda hurries out to the main floor, leaving us alone – Boyd eyes me with disgust like we've got history, like he was touched inappropriately by pizza as a child. 'Stupid fucking thing,' he says. He snaps a fist into my tasty toppings and spits a wad of phlegm through my eye slot. It's ice against my burning skin; it's hard not to react.

Boyd backs away and follows Amanda out into the restaurant.

I un-wedge my cheesy butt from the corner and stumble about trying shake off pins and needles in my legs. At the exit, I place a foam hand on the door – just a rectangular piece of wood between me and the outside world. I spot Tony's water pistol by the sink and it gives me an idea. Something I can't ignore. 'Do it, Mr Pappa-roni!' I whisper. 'They think they can come in here and disrespect me?' I grab the gun and burst into the store with such force the door hits the wall and slams back into me, but I style it out and march on, fuelled by pizza fury with Amanda locked in my limited field of vision. 'Don't move or I'll shoot!' I scream in my Mr Pappa-roni voice. Amanda drops the food basket into the fryer and puts her hands above her head. She looks to Boyd for help. He freezes, mouth wide open, hands by his sides. 'Get those fucking hands up, man!' I shout, waving the gun.

'I don't even work here,' he blurts, like a whining child.

'Oh, really? Then why are you here?' I say and look back to Amanda. 'And why are you, Am-an-der, working the fryer when you're not qualified to work the cunting fryer!'

'How... how do you know my name?'

Shit, didn't think about that. I jerk the gun towards her chest, 'It says it on your name tag,'

'You... you can see that from over there?'

'Yes, yes. Now shut the fuck up. Give me the money, you arseholes!' I point the gun back at beardy; you need to give people equal barrel time when you're threatening a twosome.

'Just take what you want, man. We don't give a shit.'

'No, no,' says Amanda as she does a bizarre panic-dance on the spot. 'It's in the safe. I can't open it. I just started here.'

Fuck, she's right. It turns out even Tony can't be bribed with pussy when it comes to money. I'm not leaving empty-handed...

'Empty your pockets.'

Boyd jams his hands into his jeans.

'Hurry up!' I jab the gun in his direction too hard, and it falls from my foam hands. The water pistol hits the floor and cracks open.

Time slows for a second.

Everything is quiet except for the faint glug of water leaking from my weapon and the thumping realisation in Boyd's testosterone-drowning brain that the six-foot pizza is now much less of a threat. His brow knits, he leaps at me – it's the ultimate Man vs Food. We hit the floor, me on my back as Boyd unloads a panic of adrenaline-fuelled punches into my thick crust and mouthwatering pepperoni slices. My delicious cheese layer soaks up the damage, and I laugh in his face. 'I'm a pizza, Boyd! You can't hurt me. You can only eat me!' I fire a fist into Boyd's beard, powering through and connecting with his chin somewhere deep inside the thicket. Amanda screams. Boyd keeps punching, but he's tiring – I throw him off, onto his back, and push myself up.

I slam a well-timed, big red boot into his freshly-drained nuts and he grabs them and howls like a dog as I loom over him. 'Open wide, fuck face,' I say. I jump forward and flatten him against the floor with such force I think I knocked the fucking soul out of him. Amanda is at my back tearing at me, so I spin around and punch her into the seating area, her nose exploding over my white gloves. She tangles amongst the chairs and eats floor. 'You did this to yourself, Amanda! You know you're not allowed friends in after closing, and you certainly know you're not allowed to work the fryer.' Amanda crawls amongst the table legs. 'Oh, yeah and Tony's not a retard, he's just a little slow!' Turning my attention back to Boyd, it's easy to see he's hurt pretty bad – but not bad enough. I clamp my hands around his head and drag him over the counter. I yank him along by his ears and smash his face down on the wood of the prep area, then give him a taste of steel on the hot plate and finally, ram his face into the bubbling oil of the deep fat fryer. He kicks and jerks, trying to get away, the skin above the surface, around his ears, bubbles and pops. His hair smokes like it's about to catch fire. Amanda is at my back again, punching scratching biting, working my base – Boyd kicks his last.

I turn; Amanda runs. 'Don't worry Amanda! Today is Pizza Insanity Thursday. You buy one. So you get one free!' Boyd's head bobs up from the fryer, so I grab his collar and pull him all the way out, snapping him back to the floor. The impact cracks his deep-fried face, and warm blood seeps out. His head resembles the limited edition Pizza Palace deep-fried strawberry pie but with white simmering goo holes where his eyes were. I stamp him good until my boot occupies the space where his head used to be. 'No more pizza, for you, Boydy boy.'

Amanda darts from behind the prep area. I vault over the counter and slam into her, sending her crashing into the Pizza Palace leaflet wall. She slumps to the floor as a tornado of leaflets settles around her. 'We could have been friends, Amanda. But apparently, you don't like pizza,' I giggle. I kneel in front of her and grab her by the ankles, pulling her across the floor and laying her out flat. 'I'm thinking you'll go well in the toppings box. I'm going to cut you up and leave you for Tony to find in the morning. Maybe it'll distract him from tearing up all the fucking napkins.' I scan the prep counter. 'Now where's that pizza cutter?' I pick it up, 'Shall we beg–' before I can finish Amanda is at my side, her hands clasped around the handle of something, the hilt of which is pressing into my cheese – a firey pain runs up my side, Amanda hurries back. Blood swells around the handle. 'Oh, shit. That's not a pizza cutter, Amanda. That's a knife.'

Amanda darts for the staffroom.

I'm distracted by the sound of sirens approaching.

At the front window, a skater kid is filming me with his phone. 'I called the police,' he yells through the glass. I run for the back, taking the pizza cutter with me.

I race into the staffroom. In the mirror, I see myself and pause. The blood on my grin, on my hands – what have I done? The clock is deafening, an alarm warning me that I've been in the suit for almost fifty minutes now. I cry out, but my screams are highjacked by maniacal laughter.

I have to get out before I hurt anyone else.

Reaching for the Velcro, I stop as I realise the liquid

pooling in my boots isn't sweat, but blood, If I take the knife out I'll bleed-out just like they say in the movies – can't take it out, can't take the suit off.

'Can't take it out, can't take the suit off,' I grin.

Panic turns to joy.

'Now the real fun starts.'

I bash through the fire exit and fall into the carpark, tripping down the steps and hitting the deck. I slide along the gravel, push myself back up and scramble around the front of Pizza Palace to the where the car is parked. The stupid kid is still at the window. I charge past him as he tracks me with his phone.

I double back and slash his face open with the pizza cutter.

'Fucking grass. No more pizza for you, cunty,' I scream.

I leg it to my car. A piece of damaged pepperoni flaps around as my legs move below me like windmills. I slam into the side of my car and fumble with the handle. 'Stupid fucking foam hands!' I finally win and get my pizza arse inside where I tackle the keys.

Flashes of blue whip over the dash as the fuzz gets closer.

I finally beat the keys and sink them in the ignition. I jab the radio on and turn it up. If we're going to have a police chase we need music – away we go! I tear along the high street alternating between the road and the pavement. Bins smash against the bonnet spewing rubbish over my windshield. Up ahead Amanda is dragging herself past WH Smiths. She hears me approaching and spins around. The look on her face is priceless, like she's just been served a vegetarian pizza. She's caught in my high-beams like a frightened chipmunk – after a curb mount and a loud crackety-crack later, she's well acquainted with the pavement.

'Worst. Employee. Ever!' I call back as her corpse rolls into the gutter. I speed away. Where to go next? Maybe I'll track down Melvin and skin him alive for trying to get me to burn Mr Pappa-roni in the woods. 'I'll stuff his fucking crust!'

The Police cars close in my rear view. I look at my eyes, my big cheesy grin. 'Come on into Pizza Palace and get a pizza the action!' I shout as I run a red light confusing a group of pissheads; they gawp as the pizza driving the car sticks two fingers up at them and tells them to eat a bag of dicks. I think about turning around and making them roadkill, but the police are close now, so I pull off the common and head down a side road to the park. My car tags the width barriers in a hail of sparks, and the wheels tear into the turf as I race across the field, ruining the pitch for Sunday's game. I could ditch the car in the woods, head for Melvin. But the thing about being in a high-speed police chase dressed as a pizza with the width of a letterbox to look through means you can't see upcoming goal posts – they appear from fucking nowhere like the car's a goal magnet. The front of the car concertinas against the post sending the wheel into my face, creating a Wizard of Oz storm of glass around me...

...And relax.

I unfuck the wheel from my face and sit back, unsettling a dusting of glass cubes that ping against the genuine plastic of the interior. A large flap of pizza hangs below my fake eyes exposing my real face. I pad it with a clumsy glove and look in the rearview – there's no skin covering me, just glistening muscle and bone like in the anatomy pictures they had at school. I tug at the pizza flap to see my neck is also exposed meat and veins. 'Oh, Mr Pappa-roni, you're eating me alive! Haha,' I say in a mixture of mine and Mr Pappa-roni's voice. The irony really isn't wasted on me here.

I abandon the car and stumble around on the pitch. A

perfect half circle of armed police have gathered around me. They go at me with their tasers. The prongs *Tssst* and *Tsst* into me with no effect. 'Just kill me,' I shout. 'It's a suit. I'm not an actual fucking pizza! Haha.'

A shot rattles my skull and unsettles birds from the trees.

I faceplant mud.

Police gather, their guns trained on me. A policewoman tugs at my Velcro seal. She lifts me open to *gasps,* and a few hands over mouths. My body, my real body, has been eaten away. My skin is gone, the milky bones of my ribcage partially eroded, my heart going ten to the fucking dozen knowing it's not got long left. My organs are now Mr Papparoni's organs beating away under that oh-so-tasty topping. Melvin was wrong; the killers hadn't vanished, they'd been eaten, mind and body and soul. My left arm rises slowly with the intent to strangle the woman, but I think it's broken as it folds in on itself and drops back to the mud. She obviously thinks I was trying to hold her hand as she softly takes it in both of hers and holds it the only way you can when you know someone's dying.

Bubbles of blood expand and pop on my lips.

She leans in. 'Go on, say it. Tell me,' she whispers in a voice so soft and sweet I feel like crying.

My last words pass my lips.

'Come on down to Pizza Palace and get a pizza the action…'